GHOST BOY

A TALE OF THE SUPERNATURAL

IAN TAYLOR
ROSI TAYLOR

Copyright (C) 2021 Ian Taylor and Rosi Taylor

Layout design and Copyright (C) 2021 by Next Chapter

Published 2021 by Next Chapter

Back cover texture by David M. Schrader, used under license from Shutterstock.com

Mass Market Paperback Edition

This book is a work of fiction. Names, characters, places, and incidents are the product of the author's imagination, or are used fictitiously. Any resemblance to actual events, locales, or persons, living or dead, is purely coincidental.

All rights reserved. No part of this book may be reproduced or transmitted in any form or by any means, electronic or mechanical, including photocopying, recording, or by any information storage and retrieval system, without the author's permission.

For Rich

ACKNOWLEDGMENTS

To Dark Chapter Press who published this book as *The Other Boy* in October 2015.

1

In the beginning the world was full of dark magic. As the centuries passed, we covered it with a rational surface that we called ordinary life. But there were still some ancient places, we might call them 'backwaters', where you could scratch this surface, inadvertently perhaps, enabling the world of dark magic to break through...

* * *

Broken clouds scudded like battle smoke across the moon. Bushes, strange shaggy beings in the moonlight, surrounded the waters of a pond, that lay like a sleeper, breathing imperceptibly, in the stillness of the field.

As though at a secret signal the nightwind awoke, to make the bushes writhe in their hidden chains. The surface of the pond rippled and dimpled as the wind played over it, stirring its depths to life.

The indistinct figure of a man appeared in the fractured moonlight. Carrying a rifle, the man approached the pond. He stared at the water, watching the surface bubble and churn, not understanding that his familiar world was changing...

The wind hid among the moon-cast shadows of the field. The pond once again became passive, like an innocent mirror. The man lay prone, the rifle fallen from his hands.

* * *

"You can't leave! You know there's no key till my husband arrives!"

"Sorry, lady. But we've done our job. We've delivered the furniture to your property."

"It's not our problem if you have no key."

The two removal men, in their mid-twenties and almost two metres tall, stared down at thirty-five-year-old Alice Harding's trim auburn-haired figure implacably. She felt like leaping on to the nearby coffee table, to make herself the same height.

"My son's only seven. He's exhausted. You can't leave us out here in the dark!" She gestured to where her son Toby slept, curled up in an armchair by the front door.

"Just ring your husband."

"How can I? You saw me trying. You know there's no signal here."

One of the men looked at his watch. "We've a storage unit pick-up. The warehouse closes at ten. It's an hour's drive from here."

"One of our other crews has to take it up to Scotland overnight."

"So you see our difficulty."

They made to climb into their cab.

"Please! It's inhuman! When my husband hears about this he'll sue!"

"He's welcome to try."

"But we don't think he'd want to waste his time."

Alice watched the truck's tail lights disappearing down the lane, then flopped helplessly into a second armchair. After a moment she leaped up again and hunted among the piled-up boxes by the light of her handbag torch. At last she found the right box, tore off the adhesive tape and pulled out a double duvet. She made a nest with the duvet in her armchair and carried Toby carefully over. Then she sat down with the sleeping Toby on her lap and the duvet pulled snugly around them. There. They would be okay. Unless it started to rain. She ran her fingers gently through Toby's curly brown hair. The action brought her a few moments of quiet comfort.

She tried not to let the situation unsettle her. But it was almost eight o'clock and getting colder, she could feel the chill creeping up her calves, which stuck out below the duvet into the evening air. How cold could it get in the countryside in mid-October? She was used to suburban streetlights and the comings and goings of neighbours. Here there was nothing: darkness so impenetrable she could barely make out the *TO LET* sign that leaned despairingly in the hedge a few metres away, silence as absolute as death.

It seemed like hours since the removal men had left. However, when she checked her watch, she found only fifteen minutes had dragged by. She was sorry she lost her temper with them. They were conscientious types and had been very careful with the computer and all the other electrical stuff. She seemed always to be losing her temper these days. But the way life had treated her it was hardly surprising.

Again, she tried to raise Will on her mobile, but the message *no network coverage* came up on the screen as before. "Damn!"

She hadn't meant to give voice to the word but it was too late. Toby stirred on her lap and muttered, but to her relief he settled again and did not wake. She squirmed deeper into the armchair and pulled the duvet more tightly around them. *Please weather gods, have pity. Don't let it rain.*

A gust of wind whipped across the garden. She could hear unseen bushes rustling and chafing tree branches creaking – an invisible world coming to life around her. The year's fallen leaves swirled into renewed animation and made whispers, tiny fragments of laughter, as they skittered up the garden path.

Another gust and CRASH! Squeak – CRASH! Squeak – CRASH! "Who's there?" Fear she had no time to hide was in her voice. "Who's out there?"

As the waxing moon broke free from a ragged edge of cloud, Alice could see the front garden gate, latchless and swinging: squeak – crash...squeak – crash... Her overwrought nerves couldn't cope with unexpected noises. Will would have to fix it. Toby woke suddenly. "Is that Dad?" Then, thankfully, his eyes closed and he slept again.

The moon vanished as suddenly as it had appeared, like a last-second hope denied. The darkness seemed even deeper than before. She felt a surge of outrage. How could he do this to them? After all she'd had to endure? Then the thought struck her that he might not be coming at all, that he might have set all this up with no intention of joining them. Some men did these things. They planned them meticulously, months, even years in advance.

An abandoned wife. A vanished husband. Just another name on the endless list of missing persons. Ten years of marriage ending in silence. Ending like this in the cold darkness. Memories like a fantasy; a clamour of phantoms.

She snuggled deeper into the duvet, tugged it tighter around her shoulders. It was colder than she had expected – chilly air creeping in at the edges, no matter how tight she pulled it. Would they survive the night? Perhaps she should try to find a neighbour – there must be people out there somewhere. But she couldn't see any house lights. How far would they have to walk to find assistance? The station taxi had driven through a village, but she couldn't remember how far away it was. A mile? Two miles? Even further?

She'd have to break into the house. Yes, that was the best idea. Break in and smash up the dining chairs to make a fire. Then at least they'd be warm. She had a kettle and there was milk in the coolbox. And biscuits somewhere... Tomorrow she would find a neighbour and get help.

But what would she tell them? What could she say if Will had simply gone off with *her*? The tale she told would seem like the raving of a half-wit.

But then she must have been out of her mind to have trusted him again.

The wind was picking up. Was there a storm coming? She couldn't remember what the weather girl had said... About to leap to her feet and smash a window, she saw headlights coming down the lane.

The vehicle slowed when it reached the cottage, its headlights sweeping the front of the building, revealing the mellow hand-made bricks of the eighteenth-century walls. Then the car pulled on to the short, unmade drive, its lights still on, revealing the chairs, bed bases, mattresses, tables and the stack of cardboard boxes piled high on the path.

Will Harding, an athletic thirty-seven-year-old, climbed from the car and hurried towards her, his anxious expression quickly hardening into stoical resignation.

The relief that swept through her at the sight of his mass of wild curls and designer stubble was already shifting to anger. How dare he do this after all she'd had to suffer through the summer?

"Where the hell have you been, Will? You were supposed to get here first and let us in. The taxi dropped us off hours ago!"

He replied more curtly than he had intended. "It was foggy. There was an accident. I was stuck in the tailback. Nothing I could do about it."

"What accident? There was no fog here. The removal guys got straight through!"

"You could have rung me."

"I tried. There's no bloody signal here! It felt like I'd been abandoned in mediaeval England!"

He looked suddenly weary. "I'm sorry. I did my best."

"Damn it, Will – you organised this. It's not my fault we had to come here!" Her words checked him. She caught his fleeting guilty look.

His temper flared. "Never stop reminding me, will you?"

"You caused the problems!" She gestured at the furniture. "And now look at the mess we're in!"

She realised too late that Toby was awake and was watching them anxiously.

"Don't fight, Mum. Please don't. I thought we were going to be happy now?"

She kissed his forehead. "Oh, Toby – of course we are."

Will wrenched his features into a smile. "We're just a bit tired. It's time we got some rest." He produced a key from his pocket. "Didn't pick this up from the agent till five. Then twenty minutes on the motorway turned into two hours! I'll get another key cut soon as I can." He unlocked the door. "We'll just bring in the basics for tonight, there's no rain forecast." He switched on the hall light. "At least the electric's on and the agent assured me the place has been cleaned. We'll be settled in no time!"

He's talking too much, she thought. A man with no guilty conscience wouldn't need to sound so jolly.

Will carried duvets upstairs and put them on the carpeted floor of the room that was going to be Toby's. "Everywhere's clean like I said. We can manage without beds for one night."

The house had three bedrooms, all with fitted units, but the smallest was no more than a boxroom and not large enough for Toby and all his toys. Will laid his son gently on a duvet and placed another on top of him. "Pretend you're camping, Toby. Just for tonight."

"Where's my train?"

Alice knelt and stroked his hair. "It's still packed. We'll find it tomorrow. And all your other toys as well."

"Can we go exploring?"

Will smiled down indulgently. "Of course. Just as soon as we've brought in the furniture." He shot a quick glance at Alice. "Nice change from being an unpaid removal man!"

"That's your own fault," she replied accusingly. "You should have got a local firm that could have called for the key themselves – not just stuck a pin in the directory."

"I thought we were trying to do this without attracting attention."

She had no answer to that, because it was true.

He smiled down at Toby. "Night, son."

"Night, Dad." Toby snuggled deeply into the duvets.

Will headed for the door. "I'll bring in some kitchen stuff. We'll have an early breakfast."

Alice sat on the floor until Toby was asleep. As she closed the bedroom door Will came up the stairs clutching pillows and sleeping bags. He was frowning.

"We mustn't row in front of Toby. We don't want him carrying our baggage. Perhaps you could remember that?"

"*You* accusing *me*?"

"You have to let the past go and move on."

"*I'm* not the guilty party here! *You* were the one who betrayed us!"

He sighed. "I can't talk to you. I'm going to get some sleep."

He disappeared into the master bedroom and shut the door. She hovered a moment on the landing as if she might follow him, then turned and walked quietly down the stairs.

As far as she could see, the agent had been telling the truth. The house did indeed seem clean. She spent the next hour sorting out the kitchen, unpacking crockery, utensils and saucepans. The activity was a relief after the stress of the move. She tried to convince herself that Will was full of honest intentions, but doubt persisted, like the dull ache of a decaying tooth.

She couldn't get over the idea that what Will had called a charming rural retreat might be a prison. The place was more remote than she had imagined. Without a second car what could she do? Will could claim to be away on business and simply be with *her*. Why had she agreed to come here? Why had she been so easily persuaded?

There was only one answer: she loved the man. She wanted to believe him when he said it had only been a spur-of-the-moment thing. But love, as always, was blind.

Will seemed to be asleep as she crept into the bedroom. She quietly undressed by the light of her handbag torch, but then had to endure a five-minute tussle with the zip on her sleeping bag. Her exasperated sighing woke him up.

"What's the problem?"

"This bloody zip. It's caught in the material."

He rolled over the floor towards her. "Let me do it."

A few seconds later the zip was free and Alice was able to wriggle into her sleeping bag. "Thanks."

"No problem. Husbands are sometimes useful."

They lay side by side in the darkness. She could hear him shifting around, trying to get comfortable.

"Hush, Will. I'm trying to listen."

"To what?"

"Nothing. That's the point."

"You saw the photos, same as me. You read the info. Nearest village half a mile away, no passing traffic." His terse manner softened, became more placatory. "No one knows us here. It's a really private place. I thought that's what you wanted."

"The idea of being private does appeal to me." She frowned into the darkness. "I hope the reality can match it." Then, after a calculating pause: "Could be an ideal place for you to confront your demons."

She heard him move. She knew he was sitting up in the dark glaring at her.

"*My* demons?"

She turned her back on him. A moment later she heard him do the same.

* * *

They were up and about early. By mid-morning the bedroom furniture was in place. Will struggled in with the mattress and pushed it on to the double bed. Alice officiated, feeling to some extent avenged for the previous day's ordeal.

"Missed my vocation." He looked around the room, pleased with himself. "Well, I guess I've passed the test."

"What test?"

"Of my commitment. To us."

For a moment he looked wide open, vulnerable. But she had no mercy.

"You've proved nothing. It's the very least you could do!"

She swept out of the room. He collapsed on the bed, sweating, deflated.

2

After a simple lunch they fulfilled their promise to Toby and set off to explore the area. Will carried a sturdy stick of hedgeside wood, which he had cut from one of the wild blackthorn bushes that surrounded their garden. He was playing the part of what he fancied was a countryman, Alice thought. Well let him be the fool.

She could see in the daylight that the cottage was at the end of a lane with nothing beyond it but small fields of rough pastureland.

"Great, isn't it?" he enthused.

Indeed it was. After the strain of the past months it was a tonic to feel the wind on his face and be able to stride out freely. It had been a long time since he had walked in unspoilt countryside – and this area was remarkably free of so-called improvements. Mature trees grew at intervals in the high fieldside hedges: oak, ash and wild cherry. It occurred to him that this landscape hadn't changed much since the eighteenth-century enclosures.

She offered him an unenthusiastic smile, calculated to humble the most testosterone-charged outdoorsman. "Suppose it could be wonderful, if you prefer fields to people."

They walked for a while up the metalled lane that led from the cottage to the village. Will pointed out the church tower, which could be glimpsed through the almost leafless trees of the churchyard a quarter mile ahead of them.

"Must look at that church one day. Could be interesting. The village is a little way beyond it." He studied his Ordnance Survey Explorer map. "There's a footpath off the lane somewhere here." He rummaged in the hedge for a minute with his stick. "Ah yes, there's a stile in the hedge. Bit overgrown, but none the worse for that."

They clambered over the stile, which led into a field of rough pasture. Toby ran excitedly ahead of them.

Will smiled. "Great to see him enjoying himself, being a proper boy."

She didn't reply. She could sense his anger increasing.

"Look, Alice, can't we just put our egos aside for Toby's sake?"

It was a reasonable suggestion. But reason had abandoned her long ago. She sighed. "I haven't got an ego anymore." Only wounds, she thought. And destroyed self-confidence.

"Please, Alice. We must make a go of this."

She let him agonize. They walked on in silence. His attention seemed to be taken up watching Toby, who was looking at the trees that leaned out from the hedgesides like benign ancestors. Curiosity forced her to speak at last.

"So, who's our nearest neighbour? I assume we do *have* neighbours?"

"A place called Boggarts Hall about a half-dozen fields away."

"Measuring distances by fields now!" she laughed. "How quaint. What's a boggart?"

"No idea. The agent told me some famous artist guy lives there."

She was immediately interested, but had no intention of making it obvious. "What sort of stuff does he paint?"

He shrugged. "Maybe we could call on him and find out."

She made a show of reluctance. "I should get on with the unpacking."

"Time for that later. We should go to Boggarts Hall as a family. "Show a bit of solidarity."

The sight of his earnest face produced an indulgent smile. "If it makes you feel better."

Toby suddenly called out to them. He waved his arms in excitement:

"Mum! Dad! Look at this!"

They caught him up. To their surprise a holy well lay before them. Water ran into a shallow stone trough from a gushing spring that surfaced in a hollow a few metres from the hedge and filled the trough through a stone conduit. Bits of rag and coloured ribbons hung from a hawthorn bush above the spring. A carved sign by the well read: *NATTIE FONTEN*. The well was fenced around, but there was a little gate in the fence. The gate was unlocked.

"What is it?" Toby asked, his voice filled with wonder.

Alice looked thoughtful. "I think it's a holy well. It's obviously a special place."

Will opened the little gate and peered into the trough. "Nothing in here but water. No coins or anything."

He dabbled his fingers in the water. Toby followed him and did the same.

"Wow! It's cold!" Toby stuck his fingers inside his jacket to warm them up. "What's it here for, Dad?"

"I think people came here to make wishes...for good health, for a better future, for the earth to give them more apples and potatoes, that sort of thing."

"They still come by the look of it," Alice commented drily.

"Is it magic?" Toby asked excitedly. "Can we make a wish? Can I make one?"

"Yes, we can all make wishes here." Will lowered his voice to a dramatic whisper. "But we mustn't tell anyone what we've wished for."

They stood a moment, communing with the well, then continued on their way across the field. Toby looked back a few times at the well.

"He's made a connection here already," Will commented.

"So it seems."

"The great thing about kids is they don't build barriers." He nodded to himself, as if he needed confirmation. "They accept magic as being normal."

* * *

Simon Lucas, forty years old and darkly handsome, but with something faintly predatory about him, sat on his terrace at Boggarts Hall with Will, Alice and

Toby. The adults drank an expensive *chateau* wine. Toby, looking bored, sipped orange juice.

Simon's house stood behind them: a rambling Jacobean hall, the latest in a succession of dwellings that had occupied the site since the twelfth century. Ranges of attractive outbuildings, including a smithy and a pottery kiln, stretched away on both sides.

"I let them at a peppercorn rent to local craft people."

With a practised flourish, Simon poured more wine. Alice noticed he didn't spill a single drop, unlike Will, who usually splashed it all over the table.

"Great wine, Simon." Will was far from an expert, but he didn't want to seem too gauche. The wine did indeed settle smoothly on the palate.

Simon waved his hand at the old hall in a seemingly dismissive gesture. "When my uncle left me the house, I also inherited his wine cellar. Quite a few fine wines down there. This is a '74. Supposed to have been a very good year. I'm gradually working my way through them all!"

They drank for a moment in silence, savouring the wine.

Will drained his glass and beamed approvingly. "We just came in time then!"

Simon's laugh was a little forced, Will thought.

Their host eased himself back in his garden chair. "You saw *Nattie Fonten*, our rag well?"

"We did," Alice met Simon's gaze. "What's special about a rag well?"

"Locals tie rags on the hawthorn bush and make a wish," Simon explained. "It's an ancient tradition in the parish. They consider both the tree and the well to be sacred."

"Who's Nattie?" Will asked.

"She's the spirit of the well." Simon studied his audience's reaction to his pagan revelation. He was gratified to see that the Hardings appeared interested rather than disapproving. "Nattie is the local version of the great Earth Mother," he said, smiling. "Folk here are devotees!"

Will Harding seemed intrigued, Simon thought. But Alice? She was harder to read. He ran his eyes over her as she sat sipping her wine. She looked up and their gaze met briefly. She smiled behind her glass. Alice, Simon decided, was definitely showing interest in the owner of Boggarts Hall...

Will caught the subtle contact between them. He made an effort to assert his presence. "So, who were the boggarts?"

Simon looked from Will to Alice. "The locals say they're sprites, a kind of nature spirit, who lived here before people arrived. They say if you respect the land and put a bowl of milk by the back door at night the boggarts will leave you in peace!"

"And do you put milk out?" Alice asked, amused.

"Don't dare not to!" Simon laughed. "My reason tells me the milk evaporates, or it's drunk by feral cats. But my intuition tells me it's the boggarts!"

His eyes lingered on Alice. She returned his gaze more openly.

"It's such an ancient landscape," Will butted in a little awkwardly. "Lots of ridge and furrow and old mixed hedges. We love it already!"

"There are places here that are more than just old." Simon's voice seemed more sombre, even tinged with a sense of awe. "They're truly otherworldly. It's an area of atmospheres and presences like nowhere I've ever known."

Simon's words had the effect of causing a brief silence, broken only by the sound of Toby slurping his orange juice.

Alice found her voice. "I hope you don't mind my asking, but would it be possible to see some of your paintings?"

Simon put his glass aside and got to his feet. "Of course. My pleasure. Please follow me."

He led them down the steps from the terrace and around to the back of the hall, where a purpose-built studio had been made from part of the large stable block. Inside the studio full-length curtains were pulled back from the floor-to-ceiling windows. Paintings of wildlife hung on the walls. The painting of a female nude stood on an easel. Simon gestured towards it.

"I'm interested in the human body. It's a nice change from hawks and foxes, who don't see why they should pose for the camera!" He glanced at Alice. "I'm always looking for models."

"You paint wildlife from photographs?" Will asked, looking at the painting of a swimming river otter.

"No other way, I'm afraid. I don't paint stuffed creatures. I need to catch the essence of the animal, the life energy. It can take me months to get the photos I need. But nudes – well, that's a different matter!"

Simon noticed that Toby seemed increasingly bored and restless. He sat him down at a large trestle table and gave him paper and pencil. "Draw something for me, Toby. Anything you like."

Toby seemed to warm to Simon. "Okay." He

thought a moment, then got quietly to work, shielding the paper with his arm, so no one could sneak a look.

Alice stood before a painting of a goshawk. The bird was in the act of taking off from an autumnal oak branch. She looked up at it, admiringly. Simon joined her.

"I love these birds!" he enthused. "Raptors are such amazing specialists. They fascinated our ancestors. Even the wives of quite humble squires went hawking with merlin on forearm."

She stared at the painting. "The energy and power are incredible! Can I buy it?"

He thought a moment. "Why don't you borrow it for now? Pay me later if you still like it."

They shared a glance of mutual approval. He wrapped the painting for her.

Will seemed completely eclipsed. Clenching his teeth, he summoned his resolve. "We do website design, Simon. If you ever want an upgrade just get in touch. No obligation to buy!"

"I might just do that." Simon offered a patronising smile.

Toby stopped drawing and put his pencil down. "Are we going for a walk, dad? You promised."

"Course we are. Right now." Will picked up his sturdy stick as proof.

They prepared to leave. Alice picked up her painting. "I'll take this straight back. I know exactly where I'm going to hang it."

"It's reassuring to know it's going to a good home." Simon and Alice exchanged another approving look.

Will turned angrily away, pretending not to notice. "Toby and I'll wander back through the fields. There's a footpath I want to check out."

"I want to check it out too!" Toby said excitedly.

The Hardings waved their farewells. When they had gone, Simon looked at Toby's drawing. He held it up to the October afternoon light, which streamed in shadowlessly through the north-facing windows.

It was a simple picture of a house, with two stick figures, clearly a male and female, walking away from it in opposite directions. A smaller figure stood alone in the doorway, looking out.

"You're a perceptive kid, Toby," he said to himself. "And perhaps a sad one."

* * *

Will and Toby stood at the junction of an ancient lane and a footpath. Access to the footpath was by a stile, which was set into the laneside hedge. Will pored over his map while Toby hovered impatiently.

"This is the right place, Toby, I'm sure of it. The footpath's shown on the map, but there's no signpost and it looks very overgrown."

"Aren't we going to go?" Toby sounded despondent.

"Course we are," Will replied with a determination he didn't really feel. "It's an adventure. Just have to knock the weeds down so we can get through."

He clambered over the stile, beat at the nettles on the other side with his stick, then reached back and hoisted Toby on to his shoulders.

"Hang on tight. We're off!"

He battled his way through shoulder-high nettles and rosebay willowherb that had completely gone to seed, bashing the weeds aside until he had opened up a pathway. After fifteen metres he reached a small gate that led into an area of rough grazing and stopped in surprise. A little way off, a four-foot-high standing stone occupied the crest of a low mound. Beyond it, grass and bushes stretched away. Sight of the standing stone woke up his imagination.

"Made it!" he exclaimed. "The brave adventurers fought through the forest and arrived in the unknown land!"

He put Toby down and produced a plastic ball from his jacket. He kicked the ball and Toby raced after it. He consulted his map again.

"There's a pond shown here, further up the field. It doesn't seem to have a name. Let's see if we can locate it."

Toby kicked the ball and ran after it. Will followed him.

"The adventurers set off in search of the great Kubla Khan's lost city of Xanadu. It lies on the other side of a mysterious inland sea. Will they be able to find it?"

"Who's Kubla Khan?" Toby asked.

"He was a great and powerful king of long ago. Way back, in a time when the world was a magical place."

"Will the king let us in?"

"You have to run round that stone three times for the gates of the city to open. You need special eyes to see it."

Toby abandoned the ball and ran round and round the standing stone. Will counted Toby's circuits.

"One – two – three. That's it! The gates will open!"

Toby staggered a little and fell down. "I feel really funny."

Will helped him up. "You're just a bit dizzy with running round the stone. It'll soon wear off."

Toby rubbed his eyes and blinked. "I'm a bit better now."

Will was enjoying his tale: "The exhausted explorers were near the end of their strength, but they battled on."

He kicked the ball a long way ahead until it vanished in the grass. Toby set off to run after it. But, as he ran, a strange aberration seemed to take place, a mysterious dislocation of the accepted space-time continuum.

One moment Toby was running after the ball, the next he had disappeared...

3

Will stopped in mid-stride, stunned. "Toby!" he called. "What are you doing?"

There was no reply.

He ran towards the place where Toby vanished. The area formed a shallow grass-covered depression, with slightly higher land surrounding it. Straggly elder bushes, goat willows and hawthorns fringed the edges of the hollow.

The ball lay in the grass in the centre of the depression, but there was no sign of Toby. Will, utterly perplexed, called again.

"Toby? Where are you?"

The wind in the bushes. No other sound. Will turned in a circle, shielding his eyes from the late-afternoon sun, trying to catch a glimpse of Toby. Once or twice he thought he had spotted him, but it was only nettles and willowherb blowing in the wind.

He searched among the encircling fringe of bushes, prodded with his stick at any holes he saw among the bony moss-covered roots. But he found nothing. "Ow! Damn!" he exclaimed, as he cut his hand on a briar.

He bound his bleeding hand with his handkerchief. It was surprisingly painful. He began to feel irritable – he really didn't need Toby to start playing silly games. "Hey, Toby," he called. "Stop messing about!"

He hurried this way and that, peering behind bushes, clumps of nettles and thick tussocks of grass, but still no Toby. He returned to the standing stone on its mound. He searched around the stone, investigated the weed-choked gateway that led into the field. Still nothing.

"Toby! TOBY!!"

He retraced his steps as far as the lane. He shouted Toby's name over and over, but with no result. He felt a growing sense of unreality, as if he was trapped in the strangest of dreams and had lost the ability to wake himself up.

He ran back to the field, looked behind every bush. He ended up in the hollow, where the ball still lay in the grass. He beat his forehead with his fists, hoping the violent action would dispel the intolerable limbo he was stuck in. But it did not.

He let out an agonised cry: "TOBEEEEE!!!"

There was no answer, only the bushes shuddering in the strengthening breeze. It was as if an invisible hand had plucked his son from the planet. He recalled tales from his student days of ancient gods who meddled in the affairs of men, spiriting hapless mortals away to mountain fastnesses and secret islands. However, these were just stories, told to illustrate some point of social history. But you could almost believe they were true in a place like this!

He looked at his watch. Took it off and shook it. The watch had stopped. He cursed in disbelief. Didn't normal things work around here?

"Damn! DAMN!!" He felt like screaming in furious frustration.

He thrust the watch into his pocket, took out his mobile and keyed in the number of Alice's mobile. No signal.

"I don't believe it!" he cried in hopeless rage. I'm going to go mad now, he thought. Alone in an empty field, with nothing but nettles and thistles to mock me. Perhaps I'm insane already, trapped in a nightmare illusion, while Toby is sitting happily at home eating his tea, having forgotten I have ever existed. Was this some bizarre punishment for his recent affair? Surely not. Life simply wasn't like that. Was it?

He left the hollow and keyed the number in again from slightly higher ground. Still no signal.

"This is totally crazy!"

He was about to fling his mobile to the ground, but restrained himself. He stared around the field as despair swept through him. Then he heard a faint voice...

"Daddeee!!"

He rushed towards the sound. "Toby – where are you?"

"Daddy – I'm here!"

Will, his emotions swinging between wild extremes, rushed erratically about the field. Toby's voice seemed to come from everywhere and nowhere. "I can't see you, Toby," he cried in anguish. "Where are you? Are you hurt?"

"Daddeee!"

"Wave your arms so I can see you!" Will turned in a circle, straining his eyes to look. "Wave your arms! Wave! Wave! I still can't see you!"

He heard Toby's voice again but, to his distress, its

sound was growing fainter. "Daddy...I'm here...Dad...Dad..."

Then, to his ultimate disbelief, silence.

Will, frantic now, rushed around the field, shouting till he had almost lost his voice. But he was unable to find any sign of Toby. He called, but Toby no longer replied. The thought occurred to him that perhaps Toby had never heard him, that maybe his son was so far away his own voice hadn't carried that far. But Toby's voice had reached him... He could make no sense of it.

He sat abruptly on the ground, his head in his hands. "This can't be real." He got to his feet, looked around at the empty field. "This has to be some kind of joke!" He drew deep breaths, doing his best to calm himself. "Be methodical."

He quartered the field, striding one way, turning and pacing back. As, once again, he arrived at the standing stone, Alice appeared by the gate to the field.

"What's going on, Will? You've been away hours. It's almost teatime." She looked around. "Where's Toby?"

He stared at her, speechless.

They searched the field together, Alice becoming increasingly upset. Eventually she broke down and wept. Will, exhausted, staggered towards her. "Alice - " he began, not knowing what else to say. Before he could get his thoughts to work, she rounded on him in fury.

"You can't take our precious little son for a walk and just lose him – in an empty field! It's impossible!"

"I can't understand it," he managed at last, "one moment he was here and the next he'd gone. As if the earth had just swallowed him up."

"You and your stupid ideas!" She was screaming at him now. "We should never have come here!"

"We had to. You know that. It was as much your idea as mine to come somewhere new where no one knows us."

"And the first thing you do is tell Simon who we are and where we live!"

"So what? He's a stranger. What does it matter? Anyway," he added resentfully, "you had plenty to say to him!"

She shrugged, wrong-footed for a moment. "I was just trying to be neighbourly."

"Neighbourly!" he exploded. "I thought any second you'd be showing him your tits!"

They glared at each other. He shook his head. "Simon knows nothing about our past. Let's keep it that way."

They faced each other testily. But they were too exhausted and distraught to continue to fight. Then they heard it:

"Dad! Mum!"

They turned in the direction of the voice.

Simon, his camera over his shoulder, approached on horseback across an adjacent field. Toby sat in front of him. Will and Alice hurried towards them.

"Lost someone?" Simon smiled. "I found him wandering about in the field below the Hall. He doesn't seem to remember how he got there. And he's wet through. Must have fallen in a ditch."

"No, I didn't," Toby disagreed. "It wasn't a ditch."

Simon passed Toby over a connecting field gate into his father's arms. Will and Alice gave Toby a relieved hug. Will put his jacket around his son's shoulders.

"Thanks, Simon," Alice gushed. "We really thought we'd lost him!"

Will found himself struggling to save face. "I can't understand how he got away from me. He's never done that before."

Simon smiled. "All's well that ends well."

Will and Alice laughed, their stress finding release. Simon pulled his horse back from the gate, as the animal was becoming skittish.

"Odd field that," Simon gestured at the pasture where Will and Alice stood. "My horses hate it. Something spooks them every time they come near. The locals seem to avoid it too. You'll have noticed the footpath's pretty overgrown back there."

"A real nightmare tangle," Will agreed.

Simon turned his horse. "Have to catch the sunset. It'll be a glorious one, I think. Be seeing you! Bye, Toby. Take care of your mum and dad now."

He rode away. Will, Alice and Toby crossed the field to the gate and the thicket of nettles beyond.

"Toby – don't you ever run off like that again!" Alice addressed her son angrily.

"I didn't run off," Toby protested. "I went to look for Kubla Khan. I found the sea, but I didn't find Kubla Khan."

"What sea?" Will asked sharply.

"You said there was a sea. And I found it! Because I had my special eyes. Back there." He pointed across the field to the way they had come. "I went for a paddle. But it's all gone now."

Will and Alice exchanged a puzzled look.

"What's he talking about?" she asked.

Will took his best shot at an explanation. "I think

he's still got his head in the game I invented. But he's certainly been somewhere to get so wet."

"Well, the important thing is he's back."

"Exactly." He was relieved there were no more accusations.

They walked up the lane towards the cottage, Toby holding hands between them.

"First thing's to get you in the bath," Alice announced. "Then we'll make you something hot for supper."

"Not tripe and onions!" Toby blurted forcefully.

Will and Alice reacted with surprise. They looked at each other, puzzled all over again.

"You've never had tripe and onions," Alice frowned at her son. "How on earth do you know about that?"

They caught Toby's sudden shifty look.

"I don't." He seemed confused. "I... I just made up a joke!" His expression was suddenly all innocence.

Will and Alice exchanged a mystified, uneasy look.

"How about sausage and eggs?" Will suggested.

Toby grinned. "That'll do, ta."

His parents looked askance.

"Ta? Where's that come from?" Alice demanded crossly.

Toby looked blank. Then, after a long pause: "I meant *thanks*."

"I should think so," Alice frowned.

Will and Alice still seemed troubled. They glanced at Toby, who looked up at them with a wide winning smile.

4

Toby started getting undressed while the bath filled with hot water. Alice sniffed at his clothes.

"What a stink!" She pulled a face. "What kind of place were you paddling in?"

"It was a pond," Toby recalled with no apparent effort, "like the one in the park you used to take me to. But this pond was very muddy."

"But all your clothes smell of it," his mother complained. "Did you fall in?" Then she added, as another thought struck her: "Ponds can be much deeper than you might think. They can be dangerous places."

Toby frowned, trying to remember. "The water was very green. I was scared of going in very far, but then someone got hold of my arms and pulled me down."

His words rocked her on her feet. It took her a moment to grasp the implication.

"What do you mean?" she asked, horrified. "Who pulled you down?"

Toby shrugged. "Don't know. Someone. I couldn't see."

Confused and shocked, she struggled to stay calm.

"Listen, Toby. We looked for you all over the field, but we didn't see a pond."

"That's 'cos you're not an explorer," Toby stated emphatically.

"I was too, years ago! And your dad still is and he didn't see a pond either."

"You've got to have special eyes to see it," he replied with studied seriousness, "and Dad hasn't got special eyes."

The conversation was growing stranger by the minute. She did her best to keep abreast of it.

"I'd forgotten about your special eyes. You're very lucky to have them. But your special eyes didn't see who pulled you in?"

He thought for a moment. "Can't remember. It happened too fast."

Their conversation was going nowhere. Exasperated and worried, she gave up asking and lifted him into the bath. His weight made her gasp with astonishment.

"My goodness, you're heavy!" she exclaimed. "You must be full of pond water!"

He sat in the bath while Alice washed him vigorously. She had put his toy boat on the side of the bath and reached for it. She was surprised he hadn't asked for it.

"Do you want your boat? I think it could do with a good wash too."

"Don't want boats!" he snapped at her. "Toy boats are for stupid little brats!"

For a moment she was too taken aback to respond. It was as if she had a stranger's son sitting in the bath. She found her voice at last.

"That's no way to talk to me!"

He looked immediately contrite. "Sorry, Mum. Don't know why I said that. It just came out all by itself."

She looked closely at his back as she washed it and noticed a large bruise-like shadow, like a birthmark, below his right shoulder. She tried in vain to wash it off. She became anxious.

"You've a bruise here. Did you fall and hurt yourself?"

"Course I didn't!" he snarled. "Don't ask stupid questions!"

She was about to protest again at his rudeness when Will, looking relaxed in T-shirt and leisure trousers, stepped into the room.

"Everything okay in here? I thought I heard shouting?"

Alice pointed to Toby's back. "Just look at this mark. Is it a bruise?"

Will peered at Toby's back. "Can't see anything. What am I supposed to be looking for?"

She looked again at Toby's back. As she did so she had the curious premonition that she wasn't going to see the mark this time – and, sure enough, she couldn't.

She stared at Will in dismay. "I don't believe it! I can't see it now."

"It was muck," Will said dismissively. "You washed it off. It's gone."

She gave him an angry, confused look. "But I saw it! I really did see it!"

He shrugged. "Well, it's gone."

"What's gone?" Toby asked with genuine puzzlement.

"It's the secret mark the great Khans give to those

who've crossed the Kyzylkum!" Will stated solemnly, looking down at his son.

"How come Mum can see it and you can't?" Toby wanted to know.

"Mum was a great explorer when she was young, just like you." Will gave Alice a fleeting smile.

"Was she better than you?" Toby asked.

"She must have been," Will conceded.

Toby got out of the bath and Alice wrapped him in a towel.

"That's enough travellers' tales." She turned to Will. "Is his supper ready?"

"Keeping warm."

As soon as Will had left the bathroom Alice looked at Toby's back again, but she couldn't find the mark.

* * *

Will was seated in an armchair, staring at the glowing coals of the open fire, which crackled comfortably in the grate. Alice came in and sat opposite.

"He went straight to sleep." She still sounded troubled.

He yawned. "Not surprised! Won't be long myself. I feel shattered."

She looked at him for a long moment. "What if...?"

He frowned at her. "What if *what*?"

She hesitated, then took the plunge. "What if it's *her*?"

"*Her*?" He seemed genuinely perplexed.

"Your ex. Trying to drown Toby. To get at you. At us. To take revenge because she thinks we're happy."

"You're paranoid! She's materialising in the fields

with murderous intent, is she? Oh, come on! She doesn't even know where we are!"

"Bit of a witch, wasn't she?"

"She did horoscopes and Tarot readings. That's not unique. I saw no sign of broomsticks or effigies with pins in them!"

His mocking dismissiveness did nothing to ease her state of mind. All her old anxieties seemed to be resurfacing. She had no defence against them. "But it could be her though, couldn't it?"

He stared at her with an expression of exasperated disbelief. "Look, Alice, there's a restraining order against her. She's not allowed anywhere near me. It was a fling - or so I thought – between two consenting adults. How did I know she was going to cling on? We've been through all that. It's over. Let's drop it!"

She felt crushed and confused. He got up and poured himself a whisky. He returned to his seat and sat sipping his drink, deep in thought. He looked up at last.

"There has to be a rational explanation for this afternoon. Maybe I had a momentary blackout. I'm pretty sure I didn't. But it's all I can think of."

She suddenly felt ridiculous and ashamed. She was imagining things. It had happened before, during Will's so-called *fling*. She was about to apologise but checked herself. Something definitely wasn't right with Toby. She felt it in her bones. "I don't know what to think, Will. I'm too tired to think. I'm going to bed."

She left the room, her movements feeling slow and heavy, as if she was weighed down with new uncertainties. He sipped his drink and watched her go.

* * *

On her way to bed she looked in on Toby. She needed to be reassured by his physical presence. She looked down at the sleeping form in the bed, huddled under the duvet. But her doubts were not dispelled. Something still nagged at her.

She pulled back the covers and looked closer. To her horror she saw that the figure in the bed was not Toby. The boy in the bed appeared to be a few years older. He was bigger and his hair was a lighter colour and not curly, like Toby's.

The boy suddenly woke and sat up, staring straight at Alice. His eyes were disconcertingly pale. His face was narrow, with a savage, voracious cast. The face twisted into a menacing sneer.

"Get away from me, bitch!" he snarled.

Alice screamed.

A moment later Will burst into the room. "What's happening now?"

"It's not him!" she blurted out. "It's not Toby!"

He looked down at the bed, where Toby slept peacefully.

5

They sat on the bed in the master bedroom, Will holding Alice in his arms. She wept violently.

"Hush, Alice. Hush." He stroked her hair and kissed her on the forehead. She did not resist. It was clear to him that she genuinely believed she had seen something out of the ordinary, but – as he hadn't seen anything unusual himself – he was coming to the conclusion that she was unwell.

"What's happening to us?" she asked plaintively.

"You have to stop this, Alice. You're projecting your own anxieties on to Toby. It's not fair to him." He wiped the tears from her face with a tissue.

"I did see him!" she protested. "I did! I saw *another boy*!"

"When a child's face relaxes in sleep it changes." He spoke quietly, making his voice as calm and reasonable as possible. "You can sometimes see impressions of parents, grandparents, other blood relations."

"This was nothing to do with that!" she shrilled. "It was *another boy*!"

She wept again. He held her.

He felt the situation was going nowhere, as usual.

But one thing was clear: he was not going to allow her to have fits of hysterics in front of Toby. The boy would blame himself, as children so often do. He had to be the positive one for his son's sake.

"We must get some sleep. We've still got boxes to unpack, Toby's toys to find."

She came back to reality as if from far away. "Yes. I know."

He continued, calm and firm. "Toby needs to feel secure. He needs his things – and he needs *us*."

She made an effort to focus on what he was saying. "You're right." A sob shook her body. She forced a smile. "I'll be fine."

He summoned as much conviction as he could. "Tomorrow's a bright new day. Let's be ready for it."

He stood up and turned to the door.

"Where are you going?" There was alarm and fear in her voice.

"To the boxroom." He shrugged. "I thought that was agreed?"

"Not tonight. I'd like you to stay with me tonight." She looked forlorn and vulnerable.

He gazed at her, at the tear-stained face and staring eyes. Was this his fault? Surely not. Just a few hours ago she was making eyes at Simon, getting her revenge. Then suddenly she turns into *this*! The thought occurred to him, as it had several times during their ten years of marriage, that she might always have been unstable. He recalled their many past scenes, the unpredictable mood swings. "Okay." He wrenched his features into a smile. "Of course I'll stay. Whatever you want."

* * *

Ghost Boy

Half an hour later, Will was sound asleep. Alice moved restlessly, woke and slipped quietly from the room.

She stole into Toby's bedroom and looked down at the figure in the bed. It was undeniably Toby. He was fast asleep.

Her feeling of reassurance lasted no more than a moment. She realised part of her wanted to see the strange boy in the bed in order to confirm her sanity. Either the fair-haired boy was in the bed, meaning she was not deluded – or Toby was there, suggesting...oh, God!

Which was the more unthinkable, that Toby had been swapped with a changeling, or that she had lost touch with her reason? Shaken, she made her way silently from the room.

Back in the master bedroom Will was still asleep. She came in and went straight to the window. She parted the curtains and quietly pushed open the casement.

Patches of ragged cumulus raced across the face of the moon and the nightwind ruffled the bushes and trees in the garden. She gazed out, as if trying to draw answers from the cool night air.

But the problem remained unfathomable. After a while she shut the casement and stared at her image in the double glazing. She felt herself sliding slowly towards the edge of an abyss. Unless she knew what was happening to her how could she find a remedy?

A reflection near her elbow startled her: the face of the fair-haired boy, his features set in an expression of malevolent intent.

She gasped with shock and turned quickly to survey the room. Toby stood in the doorway. He appeared troubled. She struggled to compose herself.

"Toby – what's the matter?"

"I just wanted to see if you were still here," he said in a small anxious voice.

"Of course we're still here. Where else would we be?"

"Someone told me I'd have to go away and live somewhere else. Without you and dad. They said I'd have to be evac – " he struggled with the word – "evacuated."

Alice was dismayed. "Who could have possibly told you that?"

"Don't know. Can't remember."

She crossed the room and gave him a hug. "It was just a dream. Don't worry. No one's going anywhere. We're all together here in our new house. And that's the way it's going to stay."

Toby seemed only slightly reassured. "You won't send me away?"

"Why on earth would we do that?" she was incredulous. "We're a family. We all belong together." She was surprised to hear herself saying these words, as if there were two of her, the sane and caring parent and the deranged wife.

Will woke and sat up. "What's going on?"

"He was having a bad dream." Did she believe that? Or was Toby picking up her disturbed vibes?

"The dream's gone now, Toby." Will smiled at his son reassuringly. "You're completely safe. You can go back to sleep again."

Toby nodded, trying to be brave because he wanted to please his father.

"Tomorrow we'll go exploring again as soon as we've finished our unpacking. Okay?"

Toby's face puckered with doubt. "Will we go to the pond?"

"If you like."

Toby suddenly became anxious. "I don't want to."

"Okay." Will smiled reassuringly. "No ponds. We'll go somewhere else. Now give us both a kiss and I'll take you back to bed."

Toby kissed them and left the room with Will. Alice sat on the bed, troubled, lost in her thoughts.

* * *

In spite of putting on a brave face Toby couldn't go back to sleep. Something strange was happening to him. He was saying things and doing things he didn't mean to. They just happened and he couldn't stop them. It was like that with the tripe and onions. He hadn't meant to say it but it just jumped out. He had no idea what tripe was, but he'd still said it.

And something had happened when he was asleep. He had dreamed he had sat up and had spoken to his mother. He couldn't remember what he had said, but it must have made her scream, because he had heard it.

He had dreamed again after that. In the dream he could hear someone crying. The person sounded very sad and he could feel the sadness inside himself. A voice kept saying *don't send me away...I don't want to be evacuated*. And somehow it seemed the voice was part of himself. Although he didn't understand what the word *evacuated* meant, he knew it was something terrible and he didn't want it to happen.

His parents had been very sad and had shouted at each other for ages, ever since the end of the summer.

They had shouted and shouted. Something had been wrong and he had wondered if it was his fault. And then in his dream he had heard someone crying and he had woken up and found his pillow was wet. So it must have been him.

He didn't believe his parents anymore. Whatever was wrong was all his fault and he was going to be evacuated.

* * *

Birdsong drifted in through the open bathroom window while Alice dressed Will's injured hand the next morning. The wound appeared inflamed and swollen.

"It's nasty. Why didn't you tell me before?"

"It's only a thorn." He pulled a dismissive face. "How was I to know it would get like this?"

She removed the thorn with tweezers. Puss oozed out.

"Some thorn!" she exclaimed, as she held it up in the tweezers. "If it doesn't start to heal in twenty-four hours you'll have to go to A and E." She finished the dressing. "I'm not happy about it. I'll look at it again tomorrow morning."

An hour later they were in the lounge, surrounded by half-empty cardboard boxes. Will, his hand bandaged, arranged books in the bookshelves. Toby fiddled listlessly with a jigsaw on a fold-out table.

Alice unwrapped Simon's painting of the goshawk and hung it on a large picture hook above the fireplace. She stood back to admire it.

"Looks fine here, doesn't it? I knew it would."

Will glanced at the painting. "Suppose it's quite

good," he conceded grudgingly. "But lots of guys can paint like that. Simon's famous because he has the right connections." He realised to his furious surprise that he was jealous. Well, why shouldn't he be? The guy was handsome, rich and famous all at the same time! "He's probably loaned it until he has a buyer. No doubt he thought we could never afford his price and didn't want to embarrass us by naming a figure."

His comments angered her. She found herself rushing to Simon's defence. "Other wildlife artists don't capture the spirit of the bird like Simon has."

They seemed about to fight, but they both became aware in time and backed off.

"Let's agree to differ, shall we?" He changed the subject. "How are you doing with that jigsaw, Toby?"

Toby stared despondently at the remaining pieces. "Stuck."

"Want me to help?" Will asked. "You've only a few pieces left."

Toby's demeanour changed abruptly. "Don't want help! It's simple."

Will was taken aback. "Thought you were stuck?"

With apparent ease Toby suddenly fitted the remaining half-dozen pieces together. "Kidding, wasn't I? Piece of cake!"

Will and Alice stared in surprise at the finished jigsaw, then at Toby, then at each other. It seemed the jigsaw had been completed by an act of legerdemain.

"Well done, son!" Will beamed.

Toby shrugged. "Easy. Boring stuff, jigsaws."

Will and Alice exchanged another bemused look.

"Where's our polite boy gone?" Alice asked.

For a moment Toby appeared not to register the question. Then he seemed to recollect himself. "I just meant it was fun." He smiled at them, a picture of innocence.

"Right," Will decided, "if we're going exploring, we'd best go now. We promise to get back for tea this time!"

"Your watch is okay again then?"

"Seems it is," he shrugged. "I've been thinking about it, but I can't really explain it, except to say it stopped in one of those odd places where time as we know it doesn't exist. There's no mobile signal either. It's like a dead zone. I've read about them. It's a bit scary."

With that he and Toby put on their coats and were gone.

* * *

Alice busied herself preparing vegetables in the sink under the kitchen window. It was a beautiful bright autumn day, with the last of the year's leaves clinging to the garden trees in bursts of fiery colour.

She could hardly believe that the strange events of the previous day had actually occurred. The quiet house and the sunlit garden seemed the essence of normality. But then, she asked herself, why should it be anything else? Strangeness was just a feeling that could be dispelled by a bit of common sense.

But Will's talk of a dead zone, a place where normality didn't exist, unsettled her. She needed to fit Toby's disappearance into the everyday world. Children were much quicker on their feet than most adults realised. Toby had simply scrambled through the hedge into the next field where Will couldn't see him. There was no such thing as a spontaneous disappearance!

But her son's bizarre transformations were something else. Try as she might she couldn't explain them. He could have picked up coarse language from TV. Or at school. Or in the street. Will had heard some of it for himself, so she hadn't imagined it. However, Toby's altered appearance left her horrified and disturbed. She couldn't possibly have invented that!

Or could she? What kind of sick mind could play such a monstrous trick?

She was very stressed, she knew. The last three months had been almost unendurable. She had no idea how she had got through them. Her self-confidence had been shattered. She still wasn't sure if she could believe a thing Will said. Their business partnership had suffered. If it hadn't been for the long-running Miller contract they'd have gone under.

There was no wonder she felt ill. No wonder at all. She was ill but not mad.

But something was happening. Something no amount of rational sense could explain. Was it her or was it Toby? It couldn't be Toby, he was just an innocent child.

So it must be her.

A sudden change in the quality of light in her peripheral vision made her look up, expecting to see that the sky was clouding over. Instead, she caught the most fleeting of movements, the impression of a figure moving away from the window.

She still had the kitchen knife in her hand. Without a moment's hesitation she rushed from the room.

6

Alice, the knife in her hand, was in time to spot a figure in green wellingtons and a dark hooded raincoat leaving by the garden gate. She heard the now-familiar squeak and crash as the gate closed. She had only one thought in her head: *it was her!*

"Hey," she yelled, "you were told to keep away!"

She wrenched open the gate and rushed into the middle of the lane. She looked both ways, but there was no sign of the hooded figure in either direction. She ran a little way up the lane, looking over hedges and gates into fields.

Nothing. Just pastureland dotted with hawthorns and a few startled sheep that galloped away from her sudden appearance. She found footprints in the mud at the side of the lane, then realised they were her own.

She spotted two woodsmen stacking logs in the woodside a little way up the lane. She hid the knife behind her back and hurried up to them.

"I'm looking for a woman in a hooded coat. Have you seen her? Did she come this way?"

The woodsmen stared at her suspiciously, shook

their heads, but said nothing. She made an effort to be polite and thanked them. Troubled, she hurried back towards the house.

The woodsmen gazed after her and muttered to each other, exchanging looks of dark complicity.

She hurried back to the garden. As she turned the door handle to enter the house, she spotted the impression of a grimy hand that could be clearly seen on the damp surface of the door. She held her own hand to the impression. Both hand and impression were the same size and shape. She looked at her hand – it was clean.

Seized with apprehension she cautiously entered the house. She was still grasping the kitchen knife.

A frantic search began, starting in the bedrooms. She flung open the doors of the fitted wardrobes, peered under beds and behind the shower curtain.

She searched the ground floor rooms, bursting into the office, the cloakroom, even the downstairs' toilet, but finding no sign of anyone. She looked carefully at the floors, searching for tell-tale signs that someone had walked across in outdoor footwear. She found nothing and ended up sitting on the staircase, relieved but still disturbed.

Had she imagined it? Was her mind no longer under her control? But no, there was absolutely no doubt – she had definitely seen a woman, the same height and build as...*her*.

* * *

Will, Alice and Toby ate their evening meal in the dining area, just off the kitchen. Somehow she had managed to pull herself together sufficiently to make a vegetable stew with dumplings.

"See anyone interesting on your walk?" she asked as casually as she could.

Will shook his head. "A few curtain twitchers in the village. Inevitable, I suppose. We decided to take a look at the church on the way back. It's *St Philip and St James*. May Day dedication. Fairly uncommon."

Toby looked up brightly. "We saw a ghost."

She was completely unprepared for this new revelation. "What?" The one word was all she could manage.

Will elaborated. "Toby thought he saw someone spying on us in the graveyard. I didn't see anything at all. I told him it was just a ghost."

She was shocked. "Why tell him something that might frighten him?"

"Were you frightened, Toby?" Will asked.

Toby's manner seemed to shift. He put his elbows on the table and thrust his head forward belligerently. His voice became a shade harsher. "Nah. Ghosts don't scare me."

Alice was too preoccupied with the day's events to pay much attention to Toby's dismissive attitude. "What was it like, this ghost?"

Toby shrugged. "Dunno. It was behind this big gravestone. When I looked again it had pissed off."

"Toby! Language!" she exclaimed, shocked. She glanced at Will, who seemed indifferent.

"Why this interest in ghosts?" Will wanted to know.

"No interest," she said as lightly as she could. "I just hoped it hadn't frightened him."

"Take more'n a stupid ghost to put the wind up me!" Toby stated with emphasis.

She wasn't going to let this one pass unchallenged. "Toby! Where has this kind of talk come from?"

A fleeting expression appeared on their son's face: shifty, cunning, devious. The expression vanished in an instant. Before they could comment on it, they were interrupted by a loud crash from the lounge.

When they rushed into the room, they found Simon's painting lying face downwards on the stone hearth.

"You should have let me hang it more firmly," Will said patronisingly. "It's a heavy painting. The wall probably needs replugging for the hook."

She picked up the painting. "I hung it perfectly well, thank you. The hook's still in the wall, as you can see. And it's secure." She gave the hook a tug. "And the hanging cord hasn't broken."

He looked puzzled. "So how could it have fallen?"

They stared at the painting, completely nonplussed. Will hung it back on its hook.

"Odd thing is, it fell on the stone hearth, but seems not to be damaged." He shook his head in disbelief. "Not even a scratch on the frame."

"And it came down with such a crash!"

They noticed Toby staring at the painting.

"Good painting, isn't it, Toby?" Alice enthused.

Toby scowled. "That bird tried to peck out my eyes!"

Will was taken aback. "Don't be silly. It's just a painting."

"It did! I hate it!" Toby shouted and ran from the room.

They were about to follow him when the lights suddenly went out. They only had time to gasp with surprise before the lights came back on again momentarily. In those few seconds, Alice saw the woman in the hooded raincoat peering in through the window.

She screamed. The lights went off again.

"What is it?" Will asked in alarm.

"Look at the window!" she shrieked. "Look! Look!"

The lights came on again. Alice stared at the window in a confusion of anger and fear. Will looked too, but the figure of the woman had gone.

"You won't get away this time!" Alice shouted.

Armed with a torch and followed uncertainly by Will, Alice rushed out of the back door. She shone the torch around the garden, but there was no sign of the hooded figure.

"I saw her," Alice hissed under her breath.

"Who?"

"That woman."

"What woman?"

She'd had enough of his pretence. "You know who I mean! She was looking in the window. I saw her out here this afternoon."

"That's nonsense!" he exclaimed, seeming genuinely shocked.

"She's trying to split us up," she stated vehemently. "People like that never stop."

He waved his arm at the empty garden. "Well at this rate she's going to succeed!"

She was shaking now with fear and fury. "So you admit it? You agree it was her?"

"I'm agreeing to nothing," he stated bullishly. "I want to see proof."

She yelled at him. "I saw her! How much proof do you need?"

He thrust his chin out resolutely. "*I* have to see her. And so far, I haven't."

"Haven't you?" She glared at him.

"If you weren't so uptight all the time, perhaps I wouldn't have been tempted in the first place!" He turned towards the house. "This is pointless. I'm going back in. The lights seem to be working okay again."

Upset and frustrated, she was about to follow him when she caught sight of something in the light of her torch, something that hadn't been there earlier.

"Will!"

He came back out reluctantly and joined her. They stared at the writing on the outhouse wall, illuminated in her torch beam:

THE BOY IS TO BLAME

"Who can – ?" She was too confused to say more.

"Don't ask. We don't know." He continued staring at the wall. He seemed as bewildered as she was.

"But what does it mean?" she asked in despair.

He shook his head. A sudden realisation dawned on him. "Toby's been on his own all this time!"

They hurried into the house. Toby sat with his head on his knees on the bottom step of the staircase.

"All right, Toby?" Will asked, looking down anxiously at his son.

"That bird. It scared me." Toby looked up at his parents anxiously.

He had no idea why the bird had frightened him, but when he'd looked at the painting his head had been suddenly filled with images of wings and talons. He couldn't say where the images came from, but they brought feelings of panic and terror.

The only thing in his life that compared with this was the fear that seized him when he accidentally stepped too close to a wasps' nest in a wood when they were on holiday. He had run away, but had been badly stung on his arms and neck.

The experience had made him aware that outdoor places could be dangerous. But he had never seen a hawk like the one in the painting ever before in his life. He didn't even know birds like that existed. He felt confused now as well as frightened. Where had the images of wings and talons come from?

Alice smiled reassuringly. "It can't hurt you. It's only a painting. But we'll take it down and it will have gone."

Toby looked up at his parents. He tried to make his face seem as if he wasn't afraid any more. But he still felt, deep down in some mysterious place inside him, a yawning gulf of terror because of the bird.

Will and Alice looked down wonderingly at their son. He was a sensitive child, but not given to bouts of irrational fear. Alice wondered if Toby was having nightmares, brought on by her rows with Will and the unsettling house move. She said nothing, simply because she didn't want to make too big a fuss about what had just happened, hoping instead that Toby would settle down in their new home and any lingering problems would disappear naturally.

She glanced at Will and caught another fleeting impression of guilt. She realised he was blaming himself for Toby's distress, which was appropriate, because their situation was all his fault.

"Got a headache," Toby announced glumly. "I want to go to bed."

"Don't you want a cup of cocoa?" Alice asked.

"No, thanks. Bed." Toby stood up and began slowly to climb the stairs.

"Okay. Let's go up for a wash." Will caught Toby up and took his hand.

Alice watched them, feeling troubled. It was rare for Toby voluntarily to decide to go to bed. For a moment she had the disquieting idea that perhaps a new cycle of problems was only just beginning. She pushed the thought firmly away.

"Was it a real ghost we saw near the church?" Toby asked, as he and Will turned on to the landing.

"A *real* ghost?" Will laughed. "Now that's a question!"

7

Later that evening and with considerable regret, Alice took Simon's painting down. Will talked on the newly-connected landline.

"Nothing unusual? No electrical storms? I see. Thanks very much." He rang off. "There's been no strange weather round here evidently. I'll get the agent to send someone out to check the lighting circuit."

"What will we tell Simon about the painting? He'll expect to see it if he calls." She had placed the painting on a chair and was looking at it sadly.

He grinned. "Tell him we've hung it in our bedroom. It inspires us to acts of primal vigour!"

"I'm not sure Simon thinks of himself as a painter of erotic birds!"

They laughed. Then they both stopped laughing in surprise.

"Do you realise it's the first time we've laughed since we came to this house?" Alice said, as the realisation sank in.

"Let's hope it's not the last!" he added drily.

"Why should it be?" She was immediately suspicious, assailed by doubts.

"No reason. I was joking. Don't overreact." He shook his head. "I hardly dare say a word as it is."

He turned away, went to the window and looked out. "It's raining." He paused a moment, then drew the curtains quickly.

"What did you see?" she asked, trying to keep the sudden fear out of her voice.

He turned to her with a bland smile. "Rain."

* * *

Next morning Alice examined the outhouse wall. She could hardly make out anything at first because it had rained hard in the night and washed most of the writing away.

Will came in through the garden gate. His hand was freshly bandaged.

"How's the hand?" she asked, noticing the new bandage.

"They gave me a week's antibiotics. Have to go back if it doesn't improve." He pulled a face. "Bloody thing hurts like hell now too."

She gestured at the outhouse wall. "The rain's got rid of most of it. But you can still see the outline of a few letters." She traced the faded letters with her fingers. "You can read the B-L-A of *BLAME* quite clearly."

He came closer and looked at the wall, nodding thoughtfully as he watched her fingers picking out the letters. Her hands suddenly seemed to him as if they belonged to a stranger. Had they ever really known each other? Had anyone? And what about Toby? Who was he? He pushed the unsettling thoughts away.

Alice was still looking at the faded letters. "It's reassuring that we both saw it," she stated with undisguised relief. "They'll disappear completely with the next shower of rain."

"Implying we only suffer delusions when we're alone."

She ignored his comment, determined not to be drawn. "I'm going to walk to the village. I'll take Toby."

"Good idea." He smiled. He didn't want to get involved in a disagreement either. "I'll do some work on the Miller project and keep an eye out for the electrician. Oh, and I'll put a new catch on that gate if my hand lets me."

He's playing Mr Nice Guy, she thought. But for how long? As she turned to go into the house he called after her.

"Let me know if you see any ghosts!" He grinned. "Take the camera – get hard evidence!"

She didn't respond. He was being jolly again. It worried her.

* * *

An hour later Alice and Toby pushed through the gate from the overgrown section of footpath into the field.

Toby scowled at her. "You said we were going to the village."

"I changed my mind. I decided to come here instead." She tried to sound as matter-of-fact as she could.

"Don't like it here," he stated firmly. "I want to go back."

She persisted. "Why don't you show me where you found the pond?"

He frowned. "Can't. Don't have my special eyes today."

"Let's just walk down the field," she suggested. "You might remember."

His voice became slightly harsher. "No! I told you, stupid – ain't gonna go!" He turned and ran back to the gate.

Alice, shocked, was slow to react. But, as Toby went through the gate, for a split second she caught a clear view of him:

It was not Toby. The boy she glimpsed was bigger and had fair hair. She was stunned for a moment, then she set off running after him. "Toby! TOBY!!"

She caught him up in the lane. He looked like himself again. Feeling increasingly desperate, she grabbed him by the arm. "What's wrong with you, Toby? I'm only trying to find out what happened when you were exploring with Dad."

"I'm going back. I want to play with my train," he replied crossly.

She wasn't prepared to give in. "Why are you behaving like this?" She began to shake him. She had never done it before, but her anxiety and frustration simply overwhelmed her. "I don't – like – rude – little – boys! I – don't – like – them!"

"Gerroff me!" he shouted harshly. "Gerroff me, you stupid bitch!"

He pulled an arm free and slapped her face hard. She let go of him and he set off running down the lane.

She was too stunned to react. For a moment, as she watched him, she heard a double set of running footfalls in the lane, saw two boys, like Siamese twins, running side by side.

* * *

Toby lay on the floor watching his train go round and round the track. He couldn't explain about the pond. It was there sometimes, but it wasn't at others. It was green and slimy and he thought someone lived under it. But it was all very strange and his head got in a muddle when he tried to think about it.

He hadn't wanted to get cross with mum, but he didn't want to go down the field. Just being there made him feel unhappy and all jumbled up inside. He hadn't meant to hit her, but he'd got scared like he had with the painting of the bird. Now mum was upset with him, but she hadn't told him off.

He didn't feel safe in the field. He felt safe with his train, but it had become boring. It occurred to him that it might be more fun if he could make the train go faster...

Alice worked on her laptop at the table, typing Will's notes. The laptop connected to a printer that had been brought in from the small adjacent room they called the office. As she typed, she could hear Toby's train behind her, going round and round the track.

The side of her face that Toby had struck was red and sore. It felt hot and too tender to touch. She was surprised by the force of the blow. That was another thing about children: they were much stronger than you realised.

She hadn't been cross with Toby. She shouldn't have tried to force him to go down that field. She let the matter lie. If she made a fuss Will would find out and he would not accept her reason for going there. But she had to know if there was somewhere Toby could have been hidden. Her rational explanations for his disappearance were crumbling, like the eroded banks of a neglected pond...

Will entered breezily. "It's all checked out. Nothing wrong with the electrics. Just a blip." He stared at Alice, frowning. "What's happened to your face?"

"A branch swung back and caught me," she lied. "It's nothing." She knew Toby would not contradict her. She fed paper into the printer. "Did she have a child? And don't ask who."

"A son. He'd be nine or ten by now," he stated with apparent indifference. "Why?"

She shrugged. "Nothing. No reason."

"Alice, please..." All at once he seemed weary, even dejected. "Can't we just leave this subject?"

She rounded on him angrily, but he turned away without another word. She didn't want a row in front of Toby so she let the matter lie.

Toby's train suddenly began circling the track much faster. Toby knelt on the floor, watching it with focussed intensity.

Alice started printing. To her surprise, when each sheet emerged from the printer it was entirely blank.

She showed the blank pages to Will. "What's happened to this printer?"

He looked at the pages, tried to print one himself. It came out blank like the rest. He tried again, with the same result.

"Probably a bad connection." His attention was suddenly distracted by Toby's train. "Isn't that train going too fast for the track?" He became alarmed: "Toby – what's wrong with your train?"

Toby's attention was fixed on the train. "It's supposed to go fast. Faster! Faster! Faster!"

The train went so fast it careered off the track.

Toby whooped and cackled with delight. At the same time the printer burst into life and started to print page after page at incredibly high speed.

When Will and Alice looked at the pages they were covered from top to bottom with the words:

THE BOY IS TO BLAME
THE BOY IS TO BLAME
THE BOY IS TO BLAME

As they looked at each other in astonishment sounds began: a stupendous knocking, which startled them both. She pointed to the wall above the fireplace.

"It's coming from the wall!"

He shook his head. "It can't be. It's a solid wall."

Rushing and swooping sounds began, first on one side of the room, then on the other. Will and Alice turned this way and that, looking for the source of the sound.

They caught sight of Toby, who sat on the floor staring with rapt attention into the middle distance, as though looking into a world they couldn't see.

"Toby!!" Alice yelled.

Toby started to laugh. His laughter was joined by many voices, all laughing at once in a variety of pitches: deep belly laughs, high-pitched giggles, harsh cackles, raucous guffaws...

The laughter came from everywhere and nowhere. Will and Alice recoiled from it, as if they were under attack.

"Stop it, Toby!" Will shouted.

He grabbed a cushion from a chair and threw it at Toby. To his surprise Toby stood up and caught it effortlessly, then flung it back at Will. For a few seconds father and son glared at each other across the room. Then Toby knelt on the floor and placed the train back on the track. He smiled sweetly up at his parents as if nothing had happened.

In that moment the laughter and rushing sounds stopped.

* * *

Will and Alice, shaken, sat at the kitchen table drinking whisky.

"So now you can see," she said unhappily, "all this weird stuff comes from Toby. Nothing like this happens unless he's in the house."

He studied her, struggling to understand. "So you're saying it's true then: *the boy is to blame*?"

"I am," she replied. "But which boy?"

He set his jaw firmly. "There's only one boy here. And that's Toby."

* * *

Toby played on the floor in the lounge with his Lego. He felt cross because it wasn't his fault. All he wanted was his train to go faster. But then something seemed to push him out of the way and take over and the train wouldn't stop. Then lots of things happened that he didn't understand and his dad had thrown a cushion at him. Then they had both given him angry looks and gone in the kitchen and he wasn't allowed to go in there and be with them.

He wasn't used to feeling cross. But he did now because someone kept telling him that it wasn't his fault. It wasn't his fault that he was stuck with these stupid people.

8

Alice, in her robe, looked at her face in the bathroom mirror. The cheek Toby had slapped was covered in small ugly blisters. She stared at herself in horror. How could it have gone like this? There was no bruising, no cut or infection. She'd never seen anything like it. It was more like the result of a burn, but there had been no fire! How long would it take to heal?

She dabbed on calendula cream, but the cream made her cheek smart even more. Gritting her teeth, she tried to wipe it off and she managed to remove most of it. She bathed her cheek with cold water and that was soothing, but the effect only lasted for a few moments. If the calendula cream was a failure, she wouldn't be able to wear any make-up at all.

She stared in despair at her image in the mirror.

* * *

Will examined his injured hand in the lounge by the light of a reading lamp. The infection had spread and the hand had become swollen and discoloured.

He looked at it in horror. How could this have happened? It was only a bit of old briar; he'd cut his hand on them many a time in his rough-shooting days!

He couldn't stand the sight of his hand any longer. He got the first-aid kit and took a new roll of bandage. Carefully he wound it round his hand until it looked white and clean and new. But he couldn't disguise the swelling or hide from the pain. He could no longer fasten his shirt buttons or tie. How long would it be before he was unable to drive or use the computer? All his plans for the future might come to nothing.

Maybe the antibiotics would kick in tomorrow. But what would he do if they didn't?

* * *

Alice crept into Toby's bedroom and leaned over her son's sleeping form. Toby slept soundly, lying on his front. He was not wearing a pyjama top. In the glow cast by the night light the strange mark could be clearly seen below his right shoulder.

Then she noticed bruising on his upper arms: clear impressions of a thumb and fingers, as if hands had gripped him roughly and hard. She stared at the bruising in dismay.

Did I do that? she thought. She couldn't believe she had shaken Toby so violently her hands had left these marks through the thickness of a jacket and shirt.

She looked closer and realised the span of the bruising had been left by hands much bigger than hers. But whose? Who could have been so brutal? Was it Will? But he didn't believe in smacking children and he had never struck Toby. The unresolved question made her almost as upset than if she had been to blame herself.

When she returned to the master bedroom, Will seemed to be asleep. She crept across the room, got into bed carefully and closed her eyes.

* * *

As soon as Will felt that Alice had settled, he sat up slowly and leaned over to look at her. She seemed to be asleep.

Slipping quietly from the bed he left the room.

He stepped into Toby's bedroom, crossed the floor softly and looked down at his son's sleeping figure. There was no sign of any bruising or the strange mark.

Walking a little way across the room, he glanced at Toby's sleeping form from the corner of his eye. The strange mark below Toby's right shoulder was faintly visible, even at a distance of three metres.

He rushed to the bed and looked down, but there was no sign of the strange mark at all.

He repeated his actions, but looked from the corner of his other eye. The mark reappeared, but vanished again when he approached the bed and looked down at Toby.

He sat at the foot of the bed, deep in his thoughts. He had read years ago about the eye-corner thing, that occasionally it gave you a glimpse beyond the rational straightjacket. But a glimpse of what? A parallel world?

How did you navigate this new terrain if reason was put on hold? Did you place your faith in intuition and inspiration? Inchoate abilities, tricky, maybe even impossible to develop.

He decided there was no map, no blueprint, of any otherworld. It was all innuendo and confusion. He left Toby's room and went back to bed.

* * *

Next morning was bright and sunny. Light streamed in through the lounge window. Alice worked at her laptop on the table, with a headscarf over her damaged cheek.

Toby watched TV with the sound turned low. She looked up from her work and watched him with a haunted, mystified expression. Will came in from the adjacent office.

"Right. Miller can look over the new website. Bit tough this morning, working with only one good hand, but I got there." He struggled into his jacket. "While we wait for him to get back, I'll just stroll out and stretch my legs." He picked up Toby's coat. "Coming, Toby?"

Without a word of objection Toby switched the TV off and put the coat on. "We going to find that ghost?"

Will laughed. "Don't think so. Ghosts never come out if they think you're looking for them."

"Shall we pretend not to be looking?"

"Smart thinking, Toby." Will patted his son on the back. "But today we're going to be looking for maps." Toby glanced at his father. He seemed disappointed. "Maps can be fun you know." Will enthused. They moved to the door.

In the doorway Toby turned back. "Bye, mum." He gave her a little wave and a smile.

"Bye, Toby." Alice smiled back.

When they had gone, Alice's gaze lingered on the

empty doorway. She felt puzzled and disturbed. She knew that Toby was filled with remorse for slapping her, but at the same time she sensed that something held him back from giving her the apology he usually made when he misbehaved.

There was a sinister atmosphere developing around her son. She could feel it like an active presence. She had experience of malevolent children from her teaching days. Thankfully there weren't many of them. But the few she had known had made life miserable for their victims.

They were all bullies in different ways. Some were physically violent. Others used psychology and mental cruelty. This latter group were more dangerous and more to be feared. The teachers often suffered from their spite as well as the class members they targeted.

There was always some form of deprivation, real or imagined, in the lives of these bullies. The causes were many and various. In Toby's case he could have felt neglected while she and Will were obsessing over their own problems.

A sudden chill ran up her spine as she thought the unthinkable: had they created a monster? Was it too late now to reverse the damage?

* * *

The village post office and general store was busy. Locals, mostly in work clothes, queued at the post office counter, where the genial postmaster chatted with customers he had obviously known for years. The homely postmistress was deep in conversation with a group of plainly dressed women by the card stand.

As Will and Toby entered, the shop fell abruptly

silent. The postmaster immediately stopped smiling. The locals stared suspiciously at the strangers, as a subtle system of signals, comprised of glances and frowns, made its way around the shop. Will noticed. He nodded and smiled at the silent, staring customers, but none of them smiled back. After a couple of minutes, the conversation resumed, but on a more subdued level.

Will spent a while investigating a shelf of maps and guidebooks. He paid the postmistress for an official copy of an old Ordnance Survey map and then attempted to buy a book on local folklore, dated 1895 and entitled *The Folklore of the Ancient Parish of Hurst Green*.

The postmistress looked uncomfortable. "I'm sorry, sir. That book's not for sale."

Will felt annoyed. He wanted to read up as much as he could on the area and this volume may well be the definitive text. "Why not?" he asked sharply. "I'm interested in local folklore. And the book's for sale on the shelf."

The postmistress looked unhappy. "It's a mistake, I'm afraid. It's our last copy. It should have been taken off the display."

Will realised the entire shop was listening to their talk. The locals continued to stare at him, but more particularly at Toby. They began to mutter among themselves and a hostile atmosphere started to build.

Toby tugged his father's sleeve. "Don't like it here, Dad," he whispered. "Can we go?" When Will didn't respond he tugged harder. "Please, Dad. I want to go."

At last Will took notice. "Okay. We're going." Reluctantly he handed the book back to the postmistress. "Shame. It looked like it could be a really good read. We're new here and wanted to learn about the area."

"I'm sorry, I can't help you, sir." The postmistress's manner had become noticeably cold and detached.

"Maybe you would let me know if more copies of this book are printed? he suggested.

"I don't think that's very likely," she said in a tone of finality.

Will and Toby left the shop. When they were standing alone in the street, Will frowned down at his son. "What's wrong with you, Toby? It was embarrassing enough having to give the book back, without you pulling at my coat. I thought you'd learned how to behave in public places?"

Toby replied in a harsher tone. "They were staring at me. I hate 'em!"

Will looked at his son in wonder. "They were staring at both of us, I suppose because we're strangers."

Toby's voice became harsher still. "They were staring at me, I told you! I hate those idiots in there! I just hate 'em!"

* * *

It was a relief to Will when they got back home. He couldn't deny the antipathy he felt all the time they were in the shop. He had to admit he sympathised with Toby. They were more than just stares of simple curiosity. It had felt like a real-life version of *Straw Dogs* in the place! He decided not to mention the episode to Alice, she was strung up enough already.

As soon as he had the fire burning brightly, he leaned

over the table, the 1910 map spread out before him. Toby sat quietly in a chair reading a book. Alice, in an apron, could be seen through the kitchen door preparing food.

"Bought this old map from the post office," he announced. "This area's really fascinating!"

Alice appeared in the kitchen doorway. To his surprise he seemed to have awoken her curiosity. "Do tell me more."

"The place names for a start. Danish, Saxon and Celtic sitting happily together! The area between here and Boggarts Hall is called Land of Nod."

"Who was Nod?" she asked, wiping her hands on her apron.

"Nod was Nodens, the old Celtic god of healing and of the dead. That's where you get the saying from."

"Going to the Land of Nod meaning the world of sleep or death?"

"Exactly. There may have been a Celtic death cult here." He peered at the map more closely through his magnifying glass. "One of the lanes that runs across Land of Nod is called Hobman Lane and the missing pond in that field was Hob's Pond."

"So Hob was some sort of elemental?"

"Maybe a kind of sprite, like a boggart, taking care of the landscape." He paused, running his eyes over the features of the map. "Looking at this map you realise folk at one time thought the whole landscape was full of magic." He folded the map up carefully. "Modern maps don't show half this stuff. No wonder kids don't know their local folklore."

He noticed her eyes fix on Toby. He followed her gaze.

Toby sat bolt upright on the floor, his book abandoned. He stared at Will with complete attention.

"Hob's Pond." Toby announced, as though he was familiar with the place name.

"That's right. Hob's Pond. It's the name of that missing pond. It must have been filled in for some reason."

"They had to. So no one would know." Toby stated, calmly and emphatically.

Both Will and Alice sensed the strangeness of the moment.

"What wouldn't they know?" Alice asked, feeling a sense of apprehension welling up from her stomach.

"Bad people lived round here," Toby replied mysteriously.

"Why were they bad?" Will asked.

Toby shrugged. "They were just bad. They did bad things."

"How do you know all this, Toby?" Alice queried, with a mixture of anxiety and curiosity.

"Someone told me," he said simply.

"Who told you?" she persisted. "We don't like secrets in this house, do we?" She looked pointedly at Will. "I don't understand how anyone could have told you anything. You've been with me or dad all the time since we came here. So who was it? Was it Simon when he brought you back on his horse?"

Toby seemed to retreat into himself and pull down an emotional shutter. "It was just someone," he said vaguely. "But I can't remember."

He returned to his book. The strange moment passed. Will and Alice looked at each other, mystified.

Will joined her in the kitchen. "That was weird. Don't think I've ever experienced anything quite like it. It was as if he was telepathising someone else's mind."

"I think you might be right," she said. "But whose?"

* * *

It was a night of moonlight and flying cloud. Long grasses riffled in the night wind. Bushes, silhouetted in pools of moonlight, swayed in the wind.

Will walked through the field. His breathing seemed loud and laboured. He arrived at the standing stone on its mound. He circled the stone, then plodded further down the field.

He came to a pond where the moon's broken reflection floated among reeds. He stared at the water. The atmosphere became more menacing.

Something else floated on the water: It was Toby's ball. Will bent to retrieve it. As he did so, he saw a face under the water.

The face was indistinct, the features impossible to identify. As he leaned closer and stared at the face something slammed into him with the force of a charging bull.

He fell forward headlong towards the water...

* * *

Will woke up in the double bed. He was drenched with sweat. Alice was shaking him by the shoulder.

"Wake up, Will! Wake up!"

He was groggy and disoriented, unable to reply.

"You were having a nightmare. You were shouting."

He sat up suddenly. "There's something very

strange about that pond," he announced, his voice filled with awe.

"You saw Toby's pond?"

"I'm sure of it." His voice and manner took on a sense of wonder. "I don't think I've ever been anywhere that felt so sinister." He reflected a moment. "Maybe all such places do."

"I don't follow you," she said, puzzled.

"Because they were part of a culture that was so different to ours. A dark and ancient mysterious world where strange old place names meant something special, maybe even dangerous."

He was lost in his thoughts for a moment. "Land of Nod. Nattie Fonten. Hobman Lane. Hob's Pond." He repeated the names slowly, as if they had taken on a new and unsuspected significance. "I believe they belong in another reality."

"Speak more plainly, Will," she admonished him. "I don't understand."

"They're like signposts to a separate world. One that hovers in the corner of your eye. But as soon as you turn to face it, it just slips away like a fox in the night."

9

Alice, wearing her headscarf, struggled to remove the *TO LET* sign, which had toppled into the hedge and become stuck in the sinewy branches of an elder bush. Toby sat on the swing, staring inscrutably into the middle distance.

Will, dressed in a suit and with his hand heavily bandaged, emerged from the house carrying a briefcase and laptop. He looked business-like but a little distracted.

"Miller wants me to see him," he said, pulling a sour face.

"Won't Skype do?"

"He wants me to look through some stuff of his and come up with more images. Skype does have its limits." He looked resigned.

"What's wrong with our images?" she asked testily.

"Nothing's *wrong* with them. He just wants more ideas." He continued quickly: "And I'm not going to see *her* if that's what you're thinking."

"Aren't you? It'll be quite easy for you now, seeing as she's here already." She continued with heavy sarcasm: "Maybe she'll heal your hand with a magic spell."

He gave her a withering look and left without saying more.

Toby came back to the reality of the autumn garden. "Give me a push, Mum."

She pushed him on the swing, her mind distracted by her conversation with Will. Was he telling the truth? Perhaps she should contact Miller to find out if he had summoned him to his company offices?

But if he had, what kind of fool would she look? If he hadn't, then that would be the end of their business, their relationship and everything. She vacillated for several agonised minutes, then decided to do nothing. She didn't want to look ridiculous. And she didn't want to destroy their new start for Toby's sake, if for nothing else.

Toby's voice cut through her thoughts: "Can you push me a bit harder, Mum? Dad always does."

"Hold on tight then." She pushed the swing harder. She stood back and watched as Toby swung by himself. He shrieked with delight. She laughed in spite of herself, filled with pleasure at his happiness. It was one of the great joys of parenthood, sharing your child's unspoilt sense of fun. She felt a surge of gratitude well up in her, to the spirit of life for its largesse.

But, as she watched, the world began to change. Toby's figure appeared to separate, like a double exposure. The ghostly image of another boy with fair hair seemed slightly to detach itself from Toby's form.

Alice looked on in amazement and horror. She found her voice at last. "Toby! What's happening to you?"

Toby laughed, a very different menacing cackle from his normal voice. "Come on, stupid! Push me!"

She did as she was commanded and pushed him. As Toby swung, he seemed to be more and more dissolving into the image of the older boy, until he hardly seemed to be there at all.

"Faster! Faster!" The imperious voice was not Toby's at all.

"Stop, Toby!" she yelled.

"Faster! Faster!" The older boy roared at her.

She rushed to the swing and tried to grab it.

"Stop, Toby. Stop!"

"Gerroff it, bitch!!"

The swing caught her and knocked her off balance. She reached out for support, but found none. She fell sideways and cracked her head on the frame of the swing.

* * *

Alice opened her eyes. She had a view of leafless swaying branches and sky. She could feel the wind on her face and for a moment was unsure where she was. Then she realised: she was lying on her back in the garden, looking up into the branches of the wild cherry tree that grew in the hedge.

The wind had picked up and was blowing the fallen leaves over her. Was she dead and being buried by autumn leaves? The experience was quite pleasant. She had the irrational notion that the gate should be crashing against its frame, then she remembered that Will had fixed it the previous day, cursing because of his injured hand.

Will. He wasn't there. He was supposed to be with

Miller. And Toby? She sat up. Toby wasn't there either. The swing was empty. She got to her feet, groggily.

"Toby?" she called. No reply. "TOBY!"

Nothing. The wind whipped the fallen leaves around her feet as she stumbled towards the house.

She staggered into the lounge, half expecting Toby would be watching TV or playing with his Lego. The realisation that he hadn't stayed with her and tried to rouse her after her fall flashed into her mind. That was odd. He was normally such a caring little boy. But normality had vanished, hadn't it? No amount of hoping would bring it back. She had to make herself face the new reality, whatever weird form it took.

"Toby!" she called. "Where are you?"

Silence. The garden door slammed shut, making her jump. She went to the door and tried to open it, but it wouldn't budge.

"Toby!" she shouted. "Stop messing about!"

Silence. She tried her best to compose herself. If this was a game, she would have to impose some rules. "Okay. I'll count to three, then I'm coming to find you. One... Two... Three!"

She approached the kitchen door. It slammed shut in her face.

"Come on, Toby, I know you're in there. You have to be fair with me. How can I find you if you won't let me in?"

She heard a cackle of laughter, which seemed to come from the area of the stairs. She rushed towards the lounge door, with the intention of catching Toby on the stairs or landing, but the door slammed shut before she could reach it.

She tried to control her mounting fear. But how? There was no reassuring image to hold on to. The familiar had become no more than a notion, swept away as easily as fallen leaves by the wind. "You're not being fair," she blurted out. "I'll tell dad when he gets back."

Silence.

"Please, Toby," she wailed. "This isn't fun. I don't want to play with you." She heard the computer start up in the office. "Toby – you're not supposed to touch that!"

She hurried towards the office. The door slammed shut. She panicked, rushed around all the doors in the room, tried them, hammered on them, but to no avail.

She found the key for the garden door and hurried into the dining area, which was separated from the kitchen only by a bead curtain. She ran into the kitchen and tried to turn the key – but, to her amazement, it just went round and round, not engaging with the lock.

A deep reverberating drone filled the air. "Toby!" she shrilled. "What are you doing?" Her voice was tiny, shrunk almost to nothing, absorbed by the sound of the drone. It seemed to her no more than pins dropped on a polished tabletop.

She returned to the lounge and tried the doors again, but none of them would give a millimetre. The rug she stood on was suddenly pulled out from under her feet. She shrieked and saved herself by grabbing the arm of a chair, but the chair instantly burst into flames.

She rolled away from the flames, but the fire had already spread from the chair to a nearby table...

She was trapped.

She rushed to the window and tried to open it, but the window was stuck fast. She hammered on it. "Help me, someone!" she called. "Help me!" Her voice was hardly more than a distant tinny squeaking.

Looking from the window, she could see that the country lane that led to the house was deserted. Then the figure in the hooded raincoat appeared in the front garden, as suddenly as if it had materialised from the hedge.

Alice was filled with terror. "No – no! Keep away!" she yelled.

The figure in the garden seemed to be looking straight at the house, but its features remained hidden by the hood.

"No! Get back!" Alice screeched. "Get away!"

The figure picked up a small fallen branch from the hedgeside. In a gesture that seemed formal and ritualistic, it held out the branch, then broke it in two.

The figure in the garden vanished. The window opened. The fire ceased. The doors were freed and gently swung wide. The drone stopped.

Alice spun around to face the room. It had returned to normal, as if nothing had happened. Toby played on the floor with his Lego. He looked up.

"Mum, I'm thirsty. Can I have a glass of milk? Please?"

She struggled to summon a semblance of calm. "Milk. Yes. Of course."

Like an automaton she lurched into the kitchen, but immediately forgot why she was there. She felt groggy and slumped against the fridge. Her breath came in huge rasping gasps. She thought she was going to faint and steadied herself by gripping the nearest worktop.

"I'm not mad," she whispered to herself. "*I'm not mad!*"

She heard Toby call from the lounge: "Mum!"

With an effort she remembered her task. "Milk. Yes." She tried to pour milk into a glass, but her hands shook so violently most of it went on the worktop.

She had to hold the filled glass with both hands and walk with small, measured steps to prevent herself staggering and the contents slopping over. "Coming!" she called in a cracked voice.

She carried the glass of milk carefully into the lounge, still holding it with both hands. As she approached Toby, he turned to face her.

Toby had gone. She stared straight into the face of the older boy.

"What took you so bloody long?" he snarled.

She dropped the milk and passed out.

10

Simon, dressed in his riding clothes, bent over the figure of Alice on the floor. He shook her gently. "Alice? Can you hear me?"

She started to come round slowly. He helped her up.

Toby watched anxiously. He seemed like himself again: a caring, lovable little boy. "Is Mum okay?" he asked. "Did I spill my milk?" He looked troubled and contrite.

"Watch TV for a bit, Toby," Simon suggested. "Don't worry. I'll take care of your mum."

Toby obediently turned on the TV. He stood in front of it, staring at the screen with obvious lack of interest.

Simon helped Alice towards the door. "It's dreadfully stuffy in here. Let's get you some fresh air."

They went outside and sat on the garden seat. By now Alice was in tears. He put his arms around her and comforted her.

"Good thing I was coming to see you. Where's Will anyway?"

She tried to talk between sobs. "With *her* for all I

know. They're plotting against me – him and his woman – trying to send me crazy! They're using poor little Toby as part of some evil magic! It's horrible! I can't stand it!"

"Are you sure about this?" He looked at her closely. Was it paranoia, or insanity? Maybe it was both. He marvelled how Alice had changed since the day they had drinks on his terrace. The pale haggard woman with bloodshot eyes looked like a different person. The idea of painting her in his studio vanished on the instant.

"Course I'm sure! It explains why Will denies that any of this is happening. They want to get me sectioned – then she'll move in – with *my* son!"

"Well I'm here now. You're quite safe. Just tell me everything that happened." The first thing was to get her calm, he thought. Then, when she talked to him, he would be able to sift the fantasies from reality. Or at least he could try.

She poured out her story, from the first curious incidents on the day of Toby's disappearance, through to the events of that morning. As she talked, the garden bushes tossed in the breeze, sunlight and flying shadows swept across the grass. Everything seemed normal. For a moment she felt that she was the odd one out – a sick, hysterical wreck of a human being. But at least she was aware of what, in the space of a few short days, she had become. If she had been mad, this self-knowledge would have eluded her.

"So the fire just stopped by itself?" he prompted.

"His woman did it. I saw her!"

"And you think Toby might be possessed by some diabolical presence?"

"I wasn't sure at first. I thought it might be me...

imagining things. But after what happened this morning, I have no doubts left. And *she* did it – that woman! She'll undo it as soon as they've got rid of me." She paused, then forced herself to put the horror into words: "My son is possessed by a predatory entity. I've seen it face to face."

He listened patiently. At first he was prepared to suspend his disbelief and accept that she was telling the truth and was not the victim of self-delusion. But the events she described were so extreme he began to think she could be mistaken. Finally, he came to the conclusion that Alice may be misinterpreting events, but was not mad. At least not yet. He felt that anyone who could survive such ordeals and stay in touch with their sanity must be a very tough-minded person. He felt a deep concern for her and knew he had to offer support, wherever that may lead. He suddenly had an idea.

"There's a solution to this." He held up his hands before she could interrupt. "Hear me out. You should call in an exorcist. If Will doesn't agree you've got more proof."

"He won't agree. Because *she* won't."

"Put him to the test."

She pondered a moment. "Okay. So how do I find an exorcist?"

"The Church of England is supposed to have one in every diocese, but it doesn't go out of its way to advertise them."

"Toby's never been the same since Will lost him in the field," she said angrily.

"That field is a *very* strange place," he replied with conviction.

"It probably gave Will the idea for the plot. He pretended to lose Toby – and all the time my little boy must have been with *that woman*!"

* * *

Toby didn't want to watch TV. Instead he peered out of the kitchen window. Mum and Simon were sitting on the garden seat, still talking. He wondered what they were talking about and why they couldn't wait for dad to come back so they could all talk together.

Strange things were happening to him. They were happening more and more. And he couldn't stop them. It was like he was in the light and he was playing with his toys and then the light was turned off and he couldn't quite see and he couldn't quite hear and things were going on as if he wasn't there. But he was.

His head was all jumbled up and sometimes he felt very sad and sometimes angry, but he didn't know why. Sometimes he felt that no one loved him and he was all alone and this made him unhappy. But he couldn't understand why he felt these things, because mum was always there and dad was there sometimes and they kept telling him how much they loved him. But he still felt no one loved him and he thought perhaps they were lying and one day they would send him away to be an evacuee.

He peered out of the window again. Mum and Simon were still on the garden seat talking. He wondered what they could be saying that was taking them so long...

* * *

"What happened to Hob's Pond?" Alice asked. "Why was it filled in?"

"I don't know," Simon replied, "but I can ask. Course, they may not tell me the truth. They're incredibly close around here. But I think I know someone I can trust."

"Did you see anyone in the lane as you came down?" she asked with a renewed sense of urgency.

"Not a living soul. And no ghosts either! But I heard recently of an experiment carried out by one of the big high street stores. You heard about this?"

"No, but you're going to tell me." For the first time since she and Will had talked about old place names, she felt a natural benign emotion: simple curiosity.

"Well," he continued, "they counted in the first hundred customers, then closed the doors for a few minutes while staff did a head count. They came up with a total of ninety-nine."

"Meaning?"

"One in every hundred people we see in the course of a day isn't really there – or at least they're not still physically alive!"

She laughed. "That's fascinating!" What a pleasant guy Simon was, she thought. He has more concern for me than my own husband. But then Will had no interest in her. He only wanted Toby. She felt crushed by the realisation.

He smiled. "I'm pleased I've cheered you up." He felt reassured. Alice was under a huge weight of stress regarding Will. But she was still able to function normally, at least some of the time. He had to make use of these moments if he was going to be able to help her. He noticed her damaged cheek, which showed slightly where the headscarf didn't quite cover it.

"You've a dreadful rash! What caused it?"

"You mean *who*."

"I see. Some kind of Demdike's curse?"

"You could put it like that." She pondered a moment. "Maybe you can help me. Can you spare another few minutes?"

He kissed her gently on the forehead. After all, she was still the person he'd fancied that day on the terrace. "As long as you want."

"I'd like to walk to the church."

"That's not a problem. My horse is tethered to your front hedge, but he's used to waiting when I'm out taking photographs."

"Perfect," she said and squeezed his hand in gratitude.

* * *

Alice, Simon and Toby walked through the graveyard that was attached to the local church of *St Philip and St James*.

"Toby, can you show us where the ghost was hiding when you were here with Dad?" Alice asked.

Toby pointed to a large gravestone. "It was behind that big stone. It had a hood thing over its head."

Did it indeed? Alice thought. She turned to Simon. "Do you know if this churchyard's haunted? A ghostly monk, maybe, supposed to be buried in the crypt?"

"Oh, I'm sure it is," he replied. "It's too old not to be. But I don't know of any tales of ghostly monks!"

No cowled monks, she thought. That reduced the field quite a bit. "Well, it can't have been called the Land of Nod for nothing," she commented with a smile.

"Ah – Nodens! For all its Christian veneer, the pagan roots go very deep around here. I imagine All Hallows Eve must have been quite a big deal here at one time."

As they talked, Alice steered them towards the large gravestone Toby had indicated. "Is this the stone, Toby?" she asked.

"The ghost stood behind it," he replied with great seriousness. "Just where you're standing now."

The view from the gravestone was not what she expected. "There's a view of our house from here!" she exclaimed. "A clear line of sight through the trees."

Simon looked. "So there is. I think it's the only point in the graveyard where you can see that far."

She lingered, looking at the view of the house. Yes, it all began to fit together now, she thought.

"Thanks for showing us, Toby," she smiled, trying to keep her teeming emotions under control.

"If the ghost had still been there would you have been scared?" Toby asked.

"No, I don't think so," she replied. "Seeing it's so interested in our house, I'd have asked it back home for a cup of tea."

"A great idea!" Simon laughed. At least, he thought, it might move things forward if they could unmask the graveyard phantom.

They made their way back towards the gate. As they left the graveyard, Alice grabbed Simon's arm.

"Look! Quick! Quick!" she hissed.

He followed her gaze and looked at Toby. The shadowy shape of another boy was momentarily visible.

"I see it!" he whispered. "A bigger boy with fair

hair. Like the briefest of double images. A kind of ghost boy. I thought my eyes were fooling me."

"Thanks," she smiled up at him. "I know now I'm not going mad."

"Not unless we both are! Listen, if things get worse just come round. We'll deal with it together."

"You've no idea how much better that makes me feel," she declared, as a flood of relief swept through her.

As they closed the gate, a figure stepped from among the graveyard trees. It was the figure in the hooded raincoat.

The figure watched from behind the large gravestone as Alice, Toby and Simon made their way back to the Hardings' house.

11

Alice removed her headscarf and examined her face in the bathroom mirror. The blisters were worse and extended over part of her neck and shoulder.

She stared at herself in mounting horror. How could a simple slap have done this? It couldn't, of course, not unless there was some malevolent magic at work. She shuddered at the thought of the evil forces ranged against her. She couldn't control them, or formulate a plan of retaliation. She was doomed. She would lose her sanity and her child.

But Simon would help her. This was all she had left to cling to. However, Simon wasn't an adept in occult workings. Would he realise the odds stacked against him and abandon her to her fate?

* * *

During the evening meal in the dining area Alice wore a keffiyeh over her head, neck and shoulders. Beneath the keffiyeh the blisters burned as if she was a victim of an acid attack. Nothing would soothe them and she could barely tolerate the touch of the material covering them. How far would they spread, she wondered? Would they eventually cover her entire body?

"How's the cheek?" Will asked, staring at the keffiyeh.

She shrugged. "How's Miller?"

"Thanks for asking about my hand," he responded sourly.

She looked at him blankly, as if she hardly saw him.

"I can barely feel my fingers," he complained. "I keep dropping things. Miller was very sympathetic. Unlike some people," he added resentfully.

Business, she thought. She had to ask. "Do we still have the deal with Miller?"

"If you really want to know," he replied wearily, "he finally grasped how our sequence of images works. Then he made a lame attempt to claim our ideas were his own. What an idiot!"

"It's a pity some idiots are indispensable," she replied. She looked at Will, as if she was summoning her resolve before she spoke. "Has he got copies of all the work we've sent him so far?"

"He should have." He looked at her with deepening suspicion. "Any particular reason you're asking?"

* * *

They finished their meal quickly, then went into the office. Will turned on the main computer. Alice looked on anxiously.

"It came on by itself this morning. I hadn't the nerve to investigate," she confessed.

"Nothing. It's wiped!" he exclaimed.

"So there's your evidence." She stood back and folded her arms, as if defying him to contradict her.

"Evidence of what?" he replied hotly. "A wiped computer is supposed to mean Toby's in some way possessed?"

"How many ways are there?" she replied angrily. "As far as I'm concerned there's only one: some being, or spirit, or entity has got into our child! And it's you and your ex that are doing this!"

If she hadn't gone to the graveyard with Simon and watched his reaction when he spotted the Ghost Boy, as she now thought of him, she would never have had the confidence to confront him. But now she had new strength from Simon's offer of support, even if it turned out to be short-lived. She watched Will's face distort in fury.

"You're insane! Why would I wipe my own computer?"

"You didn't," she replied calmly. "It was Toby." Her tone became more accusatory. "Your ex is manipulating him. I know she's followed us here because I've seen her!"

His response was venomous. "Oh, you know so much don't you? Like you know she's here. Like you know Toby's possessed. Well I don't agree. I think it's all paranoia!"

"Don't believe me," she replied with lofty disdain. "Ask Simon."

"What's Simon got to do with this?" he asked, seeming for a moment confused. Then the realisation dawned. "Oh, I get it. As soon as I'm out of the frame, in comes Simon. How boringly predictable all this is! I've had it with you. You're completely bonkers!" He moved to the door. "I'm going out for a drive to clear my head."

"Waiting for you at the church, is she?" she yelled after him.

He flung her a look of utter exasperation, then turned on his heel and left the room. She heard his shout from the dining area:

"Oh, God! Alice!"

She rushed into the dining area and immediately froze in horror. Will stood transfixed, staring at the vision before him in amazement.

She let out a thin piercing scream.

Toby still sat at the dining table. His nose was bleeding. It had evidently been bleeding for some time...

The dessert bowl before him was filled with blood. The blood overflowed and dripped in a continuous stream on to the floor, where a large pool had formed on the laminated surface. Toby looked at his father. His eyes were red and dripped blood.

He stood up and squeezed his hands together. Blood poured from his hands.

He opened his mouth and blood gushed out like rain from a church-roof gargoyle.

Will and Alice stared aghast at their son. She suddenly seized an empty glass – and, without a moment's hesitation, smashed it on the hearth.

The spell was broken. There was no sign of blood. The room had gone back to normal. Toby played quietly with his toys on the floor.

"What happened?" Will asked, dismayed.

"I've only done what your ex did. I've broken the spell," she stated forcefully.

"My ex?" he asked, incredulous.

"She was out there," she waved her hand in the direction of the lane. "She put a spell on this house."

"So she wasn't with me after all?" he said sarcastically.

"Maybe not," she admitted. "But she's watching us."

"My *ex* has no paranormal powers whatsoever," he stated with conviction.

"So where's all this stuff coming from?" she asked. "Only one answer, isn't there?"

They looked at Toby. Alice felt icy fingers of dread creeping upwards from her stomach, as if she was in the presence of an unexploded bomb. Even Will seemed to be growing wary of his son.

Toby glanced up at them, scowling. "What are you two idiots staring at?" he snarled. "I've had enough of you!"

His voice was that of the Ghost Boy, harsh and abrasive. He got up from the floor and stamped out of the room.

As he went through the door, a double image became fleetingly apparent: The Ghost Boy attached to Toby like a shadow.

Will exclaimed with shock. "I saw him! I don't believe it, but I saw *another boy!*"

* * *

Toby had his usual bath, except no one seemed to want to touch him. He splashed around in the water and did his best to wash himself, because noone came to help him. He thought his parents were talking on the landing. He could hear muffled voices, but couldn't tell what they were saying. Mum or dad occasionally popped their heads round the bathroom door and said *all right, Toby?* But then they went away again. Although he felt tired and just wanted to sleep, he finished bathing on his own.

He felt sure he had caused some sort of accident, because his parents had looked at him the way they did if he accidentally spilled something or broke an ornament. Except they looked like that for much longer than usual. The problem was he didn't know what he was supposed to have done. He'd been in the dark like he had before Simon came that morning. This time though the dark had seemed even deeper and he felt things had been happening there for which he was now being blamed.

It all made him very sad. He wished the dark would go away so he could be with his parents and they could be happy, like mum and dad had both promised. But he knew the dark wouldn't go away. It was like an illness no one had medicine for.

* * *

In the lounge, later that evening, Will and Alice drank whisky and paced the floor, baffled and distraught.

"Still believe my ex is doing all this?" he asked, angry and offended.

He rolled up his sleeve. Above the bandage on his injured hand there was a big blue bruise that had spread the length of his lower arm.

She looked shocked. He rounded on her.

"Would she do this to me? Maybe she's even crazier than you and she's trying to kill us both!"

"I'm not mad!" she shrieked. She rushed at him, fists raised. He fended her off with his good hand.

She stopped abruptly and stepped back. "This is

the moment when you strangle me," she met his shocked gaze, "and I retaliate with a kitchen knife and we both lie dead on the floor. Don't you see?"

"See what?" he asked, confused.

"It's him," she said with shrill conviction. "It's the Ghost Boy. Just look what he did to my face!"

She removed the keffiyeh. He gasped when he saw the extent of the hideous blistering.

"He's a leech," she asserted. "He's taking his energy from Toby. If he isn't stopped, our poor little boy could die!"

"The blood...what was that about?" he asked anxiously.

"The Ghost Boy's taking it. Not the physical blood. The essence of it, the life energy." She was surprised by her sudden insight. "It's a case of the parasite killing it's host, isn't it?"

12

Two Church of England exorcists, Reverend Palmer, a man of around fifty, and his assistant Reverend Flatt, some fifteen years younger, knocked on the Hardings' front door. Will opened.

"Mr William Harding?" Rev Flatt enquired.

"That's me," Will acknowledged, looking the exorcist squarely in the eye.

"I'm Reverend Flatt." The exorcist looked quickly away. "This is my senior colleague, Reverend Palmer. Your enquiry was passed on to us."

The exorcists shook hands with Will. He noted, with a sense of disappointment, that neither had a very firm grip.

"Pleased you could come so quickly." With an unwelcome twinge of doubt, Will led them into the house.

The Hardings, holding hands, sat across from the exorcists in the lounge.

"We can't make any promises, but we'll try," Rev Palmer began. "Your boy's seven years old, you say?"

"That's right," Alice confirmed. Then, with a look of concern: "Can it be done without frightening him?"

Rev Palmer responded with quiet assurance. "It depends. If the devil becomes very aggressive your son may suffer some effects. But most likely he'll continue to be unaware of the *other's* presence, as I assume he is at the moment."

Alice nodded in confirmation. "As far as we know he's not aware."

"Do you want to go ahead?" Rev Flatt enquired, looking at Alice. "It's your decision, not ours."

Will and Alice exchanged a glance of affirmation. "We've no choice." Will said quietly.

The exorcists closed their eyes for a minute in silent prayer then got to their feet. "Please, lead on." Rev Palmer smiled benignly at the Hardings.

The four adults assembled on the landing. Will and Alice in turn tried Toby's door, but it would not open.

"Is it locked?" Rev Flatt enquired. Then, accusingly: "Do you make a habit of locking your son in?"

Will shook his head. "There's not even a key to fit this door."

He tried the door again without result.

A harsh voice came from the bedroom: "Go away. I'm tired."

Alice explained. "It's not his normal voice. The Ghost Boy – I mean *he* – seems to know you're here."

Rev Palmer produced his cross and stood before Toby's door. "I command you in the name of God the Father to let this door be open!" he cried.

Nothing happened.

Rev Palmer tried again. "I command you – "

The door started shuddering in its frame, as if a madman was trying to shake it loose. The wooden frame began to crack and split, the hinges working free of their housing.

Before the two Clerics could defend themselves, the door exploded across the landing and struck them a massive blow. They fell to the floor with the door pinning them down.

Alice screamed.

Toby's bed was visible in the room. The Ghost Boy was sitting up in the bed, his face fixed in an expression of malevolence and hatred.

"Piss off! Leave me alone!" he yelled.

Will dragged the door away from the two Clerics and helped them to their feet. But before they could regain their composure the sheets swirled from Toby's bed, wrapped around their throats and tightened.

The Clerics choked, powerless to defend themselves, as the sheets wound tighter and tighter...

"In the name of – " Rev Palmer began, before his voice was cut off by the strangling bedding. He fought the tightening sheets, but to no avail.

A cacophony of sinister laughter enveloped them. It seemed to come from everywhere and nowhere, filling the bedroom, the landing, the entire house.

The Clerics collapsed on the landing. The sheets twined themselves around the banisters, pulled tight and choked them even more. Alice rushed into the master bedroom and reappeared with a pair of scissors. She hacked at the bedding until she had freed the struggling Clerics.

"You think you bloody fools can do anything to me?" the Ghost Boy bellowed. "Why don't you just FUCK OFF!"

"No! No more!" Alice, scissors in hand, rushed into

Toby's bedroom. Weapon raised, she seemed about to fling herself on top of the Ghost Boy. Will surged after her, unsure whether he should join in or pull her away.

But neither were able to reach the bed, as a violent wind arose and drove them back. They battled against it, but the wind was too strong for them. Toby's toys flew around them like hurled missiles.

The Ghost Boy glared at them. "FUCK OFF and leave me alone!!" he roared.

The exorcists entered the room, crosses raised, Rev Palmer reciting the Lord's Prayer. "Our Father who art in heaven, hallowed be thy name, thy kingdom come, thy will be done..."

But they too were forced back. The wind intensified, lifting the bed, a chest of drawers and the carpet off the floor. The exorcists were pushed steadily backwards, until they were gripping the remains of the door frame to stay on their feet.

The Ghost Boy lurched forward in the bed. "FUCK OFF! JUST – FUCK – OFF – AND – LEAVE – ME – ALONE!"

* * *

As the Clerics descended the stairs Will repaired, chained and padlocked Toby's bedroom door. Alice, weeping, assisted him.

"We love you, Toby," she sobbed.

"Don't worry, Toby. We're not going to leave you." Will stated kindly. He stood back and studied his handiwork. "Don't know what good this will do, but we can't brick him in."

He took Alice's hand and they turned unhappily away and went downstairs.

As they talked with the Clerics in the lounge loud banging began from the floor above. They tried to ignore it.

"I am so very sorry, but we can't help you." Rev Palmer apologised, looking stunned and dishevelled. "The power opposing us is too extreme. My advice to you is to go much higher up."

"Where – to God?" Will exploded.

Thunderous banging came from the floor above.

"Prayer may certainly help," Rev Flatt stated.

"A local clairvoyant might be of use," Rev Palmer added.

More banging came, louder than ever.

"You might consider consulting a practitioner of what they call the *old religion*," Rev Flatt suggested.

"You mean pagans." Will flung up his arms, exasperated. "Why not just say so?"

The exorcists moved to the door. "We'll consult with senior colleagues and get back to you." Rev Palmer fashioned a comfortless smile.

"You'll hear from us again," Rev Flatt stated without the faintest hint of conviction.

* * *

Will and Alice stood forlornly on the path outside their front door, watching the tail lights of the exorcists' car disappearing into the darkness. They looked up at Toby's window, which was filled with an eerie yellow light.

Alice, frightened, took Will's hand. He put his arm

around her protectively. "We'll get through this. There has to be a way."

The sky was clear with a sprinkling of stars. "It's a beautiful night," he said at last. "How could anyone believe this was happening on such a night?"

They stood a while longer looking up at the sky, then turned sadly away and went back into the lounge.

They sank into armchairs, exhausted.

"That was a total undiluted waste of time!" he stated with grim emphasis.

"For once I have to agree with you." She adjusted her keffiyeh. "But at least we know the Ghost Boy has grown more powerful."

"You still think my ex can do all this?" he asked. "I think we're into the pagan world here. Don't know how the Christians got a look in. They must have had some cunning magic up their missionising sleeves!"

"Well, we have no tricks," she stated flatly. "I think the Ghost Boy has complete control of Toby now and his power has become very focussed and *very* dangerous."

He looked dismayed. "You're suggesting this evening's horrors were just a start – like a warm-up exercise?"

"That's possible." Before she could say more, the phone rang. She picked up and listened. "Thanks, Simon. I'll be right there."

She rang off and turned to Will. "There's someone Simon wants me to meet. Stay with Toby. I'll ring when I can."

Before he could protest, she had grabbed the car keys and gone. "Don't worry about me – I'm just the demon minder!" he shouted after her.

For a moment it seemed he might rush after her. But he stopped and collected himself, then stepped determinedly from the room.

He was an intelligent adult in the modern world where danger lurked on every street. This Ghost Boy was no more than a thug. He would outsmart him and lure him into a trap. It was as simple as that.

13

Simon's studio was in semi-darkness, heavy curtains drawn across the tall windows. Paintings, indistinct in the shadows, hung on the walls.

Two easels occupied a central workspace, one in shadow, the other under a spotlight. A cloth covered a painting on the illuminated easel.

Alice, wearing her keffiyeh, sat alone on a basket chair. She looked apprehensive.

Simon watched her from the shadows of the studio doorway. He could see her face clearly in the bright glow cast by the spotlight. She looked exhausted and ill. He felt angry with himself, even ashamed, for entertaining thoughts of a possible extra-marital affair. There was more going on here than Will's passing infidelity. Something much darker and far more dangerous was at work.

He strode purposefully into the studio. "Sorry about keeping you waiting. Just had to make sure we were entirely alone and there were no snoopers about."

"You get snoopers? Out here?" One glance at his face told her that he was completely serious.

"You can't be too careful. I draw the studio curtains at night and set the alarm system. One of these days the boggarts might start peering in – local folklore has it that they were imbued with insatiable curiosity! There's always a chance they might not like what they see!"

She forced herself to smile at his joke. He suddenly stepped to one side, as if he was a footman anticipating the arrival of local aristocracy. She almost expected him to bow.

"It's time for you to meet Ingrid," he announced. "A local farmer and tenant from the village."

A tall woman approached the spotlit area. She was dressed in a dark hooded raincoat. Alice stood up with a gasp of dismay. Ingrid threw back her hood, to reveal herself as a striking woman of fifty with long greying-blonde hair.

"You've seen me before, I think." Her voice was surprisingly deep and resonant. Both voice and appearance proclaimed her to be a woman of great dignity and authority.

Alice struggled with her shock and confusion. It took her a while to gain control of her emotions. "Oh, I... I thought you were someone else. Please...forgive me."

Simon and Ingrid shared the briefest of knowing glances. "I've just realised who you thought she was." He looked contrite and a little embarrassed. "If I'd made the connection sooner, you'd have been spared some unnecessary suffering. But I think we can safely consign a certain *ex* to history and now focus on the main issue of saving Toby."

Alice felt an enormous pressure lifting away from her. As she recovered from her surprise about Ingrid's identity, she was beset by guilt over Will. No wonder he had reacted with such hostility when she had bombarded him with her accusations. Although she felt relieved that one nightmare had ended, she knew they still had the greater task ahead of them. But at least now she had the support of others.

She returned to the basket chair. Ingrid perched opposite on an old wooden trunk. Simon sat cross-legged on a floor cushion. Both he and Alice fixed their attention on Ingrid.

"I have what's called the second sight. It runs in my family." Ingrid studied her listeners. "I've been taking note of events. I foresaw a little of what's happened."

"You left the message *the boy is to blame*...?" Alice asked.

"I knew the Boy in Hob's Pond was restless and it would only take an unwitting act to release him. Your son was the trigger."

Ingrid's comment left Alice confused. "The Boy in Hob's Pond? You mean someone who drowned?"

Ingrid studied Alice for some moments before she replied, as if she was assessing her questioner's ability to cope with her revelations. "I *saw* him grab your son and pull him into the water. That is, I mean this in a psychic or astral sense. Your son was the victim of an attack on the astral plane."

"But it must have been a physical attack," Alice objected. "My son was wet through."

"Your son was pulled into another realm. The medium at the interface between that realm and this is water. Although you can't see Hob's Pond with your physical eyes, I can see it as it used to be, before it was filled in. It still has the shadow, or memory, of physical substance. Your son had to come back through the shadow substance to re-enter this world."

Alice was confused. "But he came back hundreds of yards away in a different field!"

"You were lucky. Otherworld water doesn't obey our laws of time and space." Ingrid smiled grimly. "Your son could have been found floating in the Trent or stuck in the Humber mud at low tide!"

Alice sat very still, allowing Ingrid's words to sink in. "I think my son is possessed. Can you cure him?"

Again, Ingrid took her time before replying. Alice had the impression that conversation for this woman was like an act of divination: she had to plumb the depths of the western lexicon, so that when she spoke it was with accuracy and authority.

"We must bind the Boy," she said at last. "Confine his power while we're still able and send him back to Hob's Pond. It's going to be very difficult, but there is no other way to liberate your son."

Simon clarified. "Ingrid means to bind this Ghost Boy symbolically, or magically."

"Leave the binding to me." Ingrid turned her unwavering gaze on to Alice. "You need to be at the pond at the right moment. You know the place, I believe."

"But there's no pond there now," Alice objected. "At least, I can't see it."

Ingrid smiled enigmatically. "You'll see it. All in due course."

Simon offered a cautionary comment: "There are people here who wouldn't want Ingrid talking to an outsider like this."

"Not even to help an innocent child?" Alice asked in surprise.

Ingrid studied Alice for a few moments. "It's a long story," she said at last.

* * *

With some trepidation Will unlocked Toby's bedroom door and turned on the night light. To his relief the Ghost Boy was not in evidence and Toby seemed to be sleeping.

Will sat on the edge of Toby's bed. At first, he was uncertain how to begin, then suddenly it was obvious.

"I don't know if you can hear me, but I hope you can." He spoke quietly and firmly, choosing his words with care. "I want to appeal to you to leave my son alone and go back to where you came from."

Toby continued sleeping. The Ghost Boy did not appear. Had he realised his presence wasn't wanted? Had he gone as mysteriously as he had arrived? But he had to play safe and assume he was still there, biding his time until...until what? Why was he here? What was his motive? Will realised there was so much he didn't know. He got up and began to pace the room.

"What do you hope to achieve now you're here? You must see there's nothing you can gain." He addressed the sleeping form of his son in the bed. "You must return to the world of those who lived here before and who have moved on."

He paused. There was no movement in the bed, no sound except Toby's gentle breathing. He began again to pace the room.

"You must go back to the Land of Nod, where the Lord of the Dead – the great Nodens – presides."

He began to sweat with tension. He looked down

at Toby who, though he seemed very pale, appeared to be deeply asleep.

* * *

In the studio, Alice and Simon listened as Ingrid told her tale. Once or twice an owl hooted in the woods and a vixen squalled nearby. These sounds from the natural world were comforting to Alice. What could be so terrible in a world of innocent wild creatures? Were there really dark powers hidden in the landscape?

Ingrid began her account of events. "Back in the wartime we had evacuees from the city. We didn't want them, but the government said we had to take them."

The word *evacuee* gave Alice a jolt. With a shock she realised Toby had been picking up the Ghost Boy's thoughts and emotions right from the start.

"What year are we talking about?" Simon asked.

"It was 1941. A port city thirty miles away was being bombed every night, but we still didn't want to take their kids."

"Why on earth not?" Alice looked at Ingrid with undisguised disapproval.

Ingrid appeared reluctant to justify the local community's attitude. After a lengthy silence she seemed to relent. "We're farmers here. And these kids hadn't even seen a cow before. What use were they to us? And there were those here who followed the old ways and didn't want any Christians intruding into their world. They even resisted the appointment of vicars to the village church. Those who did take up the post never stayed long."

"But the evacuees still came?" Alice's question broke another lengthy silence.

"Oh yes, they came. But, after a while, we thought we'd turn it to our advantage."

"*We* meaning an earlier generation?" Simon prompted.

"It was my grandparents' time," Ingrid explained. "My mother was a girl of twelve and she saw what happened."

Ingrid suddenly seemed to dry up. Alice and Simon shifted uneasily; his visitor appeared to be in a light trance, as if she was waiting for some kind of spirit guidance before she spoke again.

Eventually she sighed and recommenced her tale. "I had to wait until my mother was on her deathbed before she told me about it."

* * *

In Toby's bedroom, Will continued to pace the floor. Toby still slept. Will's struggle to find the right words went on.

"So what I'm trying to do is get you to see that this has all been a mistake. You've come to the wrong world where you don't belong."

He paced again, then stopped by the bed. The whole thing was beginning to feel ridiculous. Was there anybody there? Could this so-called entity actually hear him?

He recalled the failed exorcism and the force the Ghost Boy raised against them. He remembered his scepticism and the fact that, as soon as he saw the Ghost Boy for himself, his disbelief vanished like a fantasy. Was reality so provisional? Did it exist only in an agreed cultural mindset? Was our modern view of life an encumbrance?

Pushing his doubts aside, he carried on. "I'm not blaming you for this. It was just some kind of unfortunate accident. And now it's time for you to go back. You can see that you have to go back, can't you?"

There was no response from the figure in the bed. Toby seemed still to be fast asleep. Again, Will felt the clash of realities, as he addressed an otherworld entity in a child's ordinary bedroom. The task he had set himself suddenly seemed impossible.

"Please be reasonable," he went on. "You're not being fair to my son." He sat on the bed and gently stroked Toby's hair. "He wants his life back, so please leave him alone."

A moaning sound began. Will, startled, stopped speaking. The sound was not coming from Toby, who still appeared to be asleep.

The moaning intensified, with an added edge of angry hostility. Toby stirred slightly. Will, suddenly afraid, watched him.

14

Simon handed out glasses of wine as they took a brief break from Ingrid's narrative. They drank the wine in silence, unable to break the spell Ingrid's story had cast over them. After a while, she seemed ready to continue.

"There was one boy who everyone hated. He was about ten years old and should have known better. He wouldn't help with the farm work. He was a thief and a liar and no one could trust him." She studied her listeners' faces. "And he was destructive. He'd break things, burn things. So some folk decided they'd had enough."

"Perhaps he was just unhappy?" Alice suggested.

"Maybe he was. No doubt he'd had a bad time in the city. No doubt he was poor and half starved. But the other city kids had suffered deprivations too and they were no trouble. Anyway, people back then weren't inclined to be comforters." She caught Alice's sharp glance of disapproval. "You can think what you like of my people. If you had lived through those times, you'd understand how hard they were."

Alice felt chastened. She had not lived through

those terrible years. She wondered how she would have felt if she had. Would she have been desensitised by them? It was a pointless question; she would never know. For this reason, she felt she should try to suspend judgement.

Ingrid looked at Alice and Simon. She took a deep breath, as if she had reached the crux of her story.

"Crop yields were decreasing. The old folk thought they'd offer the boy as a sacrifice to the earth spirits, so the land would come again into good heart."

Simon had half anticipated Ingrid's disclosure. From hints his uncle had dropped over the years, he had grasped that the parish was a rare pagan enclave that made its own rules and followed time-honoured folk traditions. The fact that they had a Christian church in the parish had barely altered anything. The locals were buried in the church graveyard because they considered it still to be a pagan site. Some of them even attended services, but these were more in the form of a friendly chat about countryside issues, rather than hymn singing, prayers and readings from the bible.

Not that the locals flaunted their beliefs; the opposite was the case and strict secrecy prevailed. He suspected that much of rural England was once like that, probably in the centuries before the Reformation and undoubtedly in the pre-Norman world. He increasingly felt it was a privilege to be lord of the manor here. He certainly admired the local people for the care they took of the land. And it wasn't because of an imagined threat from boggarts! It was simply that they loved it.

Ingrid's revelation shook Alice to the core. She had no experience of paganism and very little of any form of country living. She was a product of suburbia, unlike Will, who had worked on farms in his village-based youth. She had no idea about rural values, or the pressures that small farming communities had to face. So a matter-of-fact reference to a human sacrifice was a massive shock, challenging every civilised value she had taken for granted.

Then Ingrid began, in a voice filled with calm authority, to describe events that took place during the war in their quiet farming community, but Alice felt she could have been talking about the plot of a Gothic novel.

She pictured the scene in sepia tones. They seemed to fit the context and the strange remove of this remote-seeming community. Sepia and twilight for an earthy tale of violence and magic...

The mesmeric quality of Ingrid's story continued. "They decided to give the boy to Hob and the earth spirits as a token of their devotion to the old ways."

Just a plain, unqualified statement, Alice thought, as if reality for these people was utterly different from her own. She thought of Will's comments after his dream about Hob's Pond. Yes, she thought, these people live in a separate world.

In spite of her reluctance, Alice found her imagination transported by Ingrid's words to that other time. In the sepia-toned half light she saw ragged clouds racing past a newly-risen moon. Wild hedgeside trees tossed in the wind...

She saw the indistinct figure of a boy with fair hair, dressed in short trousers and a grimy tunic shirt, vault a small gate into a field. Half a dozen farm men with shotguns, dogs and a large hawk pursued him.

The boy fled from them, but found his way barred

by a big pond. The pond's surface rippled and dimpled. Bushes on the bank trembled in the wind.

Before the boy could decide what to do, his pursuers had him surrounded. The dogs and the hawk hemmed him in. The dogs barked and snarled. The hawk dived at him. The terrified boy struggled in vain as hands grabbed his legs and upper arms.

Alice heard Ingrid's voice as it added the final grim details. "The boy was given to Hob and the earth spirits, to remain in their world between the living and the dead. But now he's escaped and he's using your child."

In her mind, Alice saw the men throw the boy into the pond. Then she pictured, from Ingrid's description, three local women standing by the water chanting spells. Ingrid's mother, a girl of twelve, wrapped in a coarse woollen overcoat, watched from the bushes.

"And so we must return him," Ingrid said, as if she was describing an unsatisfactory young breeding bull, "we must return him so we keep faith with the earth spirits."

Alice realised Ingrid's tale had ended. She felt exhausted. Suddenly she recalled Toby's comments about Hob's Pond when he had come back with Will from their visit to the village post office.

"Why was the pond filled in?" she asked.

Ingrid looked surprised, as if the subject had never occurred to her. "To hide the deed, I assume. And cover any troubled consciences."

But did these people really have consciences, Alice wondered. "Didn't anyone ever look for the boy?" she asked.

"The country was at war," Ingrid replied. "We

heard the boy's father was missing and his mother had been killed in a bombing raid."

"But it was murder!" Alice exclaimed.

Ingrid remained unperturbed. "The old folks here saw it as a means to an end. Death was everywhere back then."

A jarring idea surged into Alice's mind. "Are you helping us, or are we just a part of your own dark schemes?"

"Both, I think," Ingrid replied calmly. "And our so-called *schemes* are only as dark as you choose to make them."

Alice, undaunted, ploughed on. She had more concerns: "How is it this boy has such power?"

"Dwellers between the worlds are in the realm of *force*, so they gain power," Ingrid explained. "Anyone who comes here from that world is not subject to physical laws and can be very dangerous."

"Why did the boy seize his chance to come back?" Simon asked.

"For revenge, I think. And he might still have a hankering for life in the physical world. He just saw his opportunity and used your son." Ingrid gave Alice a long appraising look. "Evil often attaches itself to the innocent. To the most vulnerable. They are what you might call today a soft target. Those who are more self-aware, who protect themselves by a subconscious vigilance, are much harder to invade."

* * *

In Toby's bedroom the moaning grew louder. The sound rose to a higher frequency and kept on climbing. Will pressed his hands to his ears as he struggled to endure it.

To his horror he watched as the Ghost Boy almost completely detached himself from Toby's sleeping form.

The Ghost Boy, his face contorted with rage, appeared to fling something at Will, who was not aware of any physical object leaving the boy's hand, but the effect of the violent action was extreme.

He was hurled backwards as if by a colossal force of energy, which slammed him into the bedroom wall. He collapsed, unconscious.

The Ghost Boy merged again with Toby. As if filled with an eerie non-physical energy, Toby rose from his bed like an automaton and left the room.

* * *

In the studio Alice, Simon and Ingrid were on their feet preparing for action. Ingrid removed the cloth from the painting on the easel.

A painting of the Ghost Boy was revealed, the figure not much more than an outline, containing only minimal detail.

Alice looked at the painting. "It's very simplistic. It could be anyone."

"It's the *idea* of him," Simon explained. "Ingrid pointed out that the details don't ultimately matter as much as the *intent*."

"This is more than enough for me," Ingrid assured them.

Her manner changed abruptly, acquiring a sudden added urgency, as if some new perception had entered her awareness. "The Boy has begun to move. I can feel it, but I can't *see* him clearly. Go now and follow him. I'll stay and prepare the binding to shackle his power."

"Why don't you just burn the painting? Or hit it with an axe?" Alice asked.

"Any violent action would harm your son," Ingrid explained. "The two boys are one until we can separate them."

Simon turned to Alice. "Can you ride?"

"It's been a while," she replied, "but yes, I can."

"Good. Let's go."

They hurried from the studio, leaving Ingrid alone. She went to a holdall and took out a bundle wrapped in sacking.

She addressed the painting: "You're circumscribed already, Boy. And I will hold you there."

* * *

Will came round slowly. He struggled to his feet and limped towards the bed.

"Toby?" he queried. "You all right?"

He pulled back the covers. No Toby.

"Toby?"

No response.

Alarmed, he rushed from the room.

He emerged on to the landing and stopped in shock. Fire licked its way up the stairs towards him...

He recalled Alice's smashing of the glass to break the spell of Toby's bleeding. He grabbed a vase that stood on a small landing table and smashed it against the wall.

Nothing happened.

He remembered the failed exorcism and realised that the Ghost Boy's power seemed to have grown considerably since the evening when Alice had smashed the glass. It was now too great for him to oppose.

He watched helplessly as the fire spread to the landing. "I can't stop it!" he exclaimed, as perspiration burst out on his forehead. It dawned on him that this was no phantom fire. It was real.

He hurried into the master bedroom and grabbed the extension telephone, but the line was dead. "Damn!"

He returned to the landing. The fire was already approaching Toby's bedroom door. He hesitated, trying to decide what to do. Images from his life flashed through his mind. So many crises! And they were still coming at him! Was this it – was he going to succumb this time? No! Definitely no!

He turned back into the master bedroom, reappearing a moment later with a blanket.

A newspaper headline flashed across him mind: *Man Burnt to Death in Cottage*. "I don't think so!" he yelled. "I DON'T THINK SO!"

Using the blanket, he attempted to smother the advancing flames. Slowly he worked his way along the landing...

15

The full moon was hidden behind a dappled layer of altocumulus, but there was enough light to see by filtering through the cloud. A fitful breeze hissed in the leafless hedges as Alice and Simon, on horseback, rode through the maze of lanes that crisscrossed the rural parish.

"We should start at your place," he remarked. "Then work outwards from there. Toby might still be in the house."

"What will we do if he isn't?" she asked anxiously.

"If Ingrid's right, and this Ghost Boy's after revenge, there'll be signs," he replied, grimly. "She gave us fairly clear hints of his *modus operandi*."

He turned his horse on to a narrow lane, hardly more than a cart track. She lost her sense of direction immediately.

"How does anyone remember where they are down here?" she asked in confusion. "I thought I knew where we were, but I was obviously wrong. All these lanes look the same, especially in the dark."

"This is a short cut," he explained. "It took me a full year to figure these lanes out in the daylight. I still occasionally get lost at night." He uttered a self-deprecating chuckle. " If I'm out riding, my horses always know where they are, so I just have to say *let's go home*!"

He was surprised to hear her laugh. If it hadn't been for the extreme situation they were caught up in, he would have made a more intimate comment at this point. There was no doubt he felt attracted to this feisty and determined woman and he felt that his interest was returned.

But this was, to say the least, an unusual situation that had pretty much hurled them together. In normal circumstances, whatever *they* were, would he and Alice feel the same? He decided there was a strong chance they would; that was, of course, if normality could ever be induced to return.

She knew he was giving her sidelong glances as they rode down the lane in the moonlight. At her first meeting with him there had been a moment when she had quite fancied him and might have risked throwing herself into an affair to get her revenge on Will. But this wasn't going to happen – even if Will hadn't, after all, been conspiring with his ex – until Toby was separated, undamaged from the grip of the Ghost Boy.

Simon suddenly grabbed her arm and pointed. "There's a fire! And it's over your way!"

They spurred their mounts in the direction of the fire. They could clearly see the glow in the sky above the tops of the field hedges, which suggested it was a sizeable blaze. When they turned the last corner, they could hear the roar of the flames and saw that the house was burning fiercely.

"I have to get in there!" she cried.

He turned his horse in front of hers, blocking her

advance, then grabbed her reins. "It's a death trap! I won't let you! You wouldn't survive it!"

She was distraught. "What about Toby and Will?"

He pointed. A second fire, half a mile away over the fields, had caught his attention. "Some revenge!" he exclaimed. He turned to her. "As long as the Ghost Boy is active, Toby has to be with him. As we now know the Boy can only materialise through Toby's life energy." He was relieved to see that his point had sunk in. He pushed the thought away of what would happen if the Ghost Boy used up Toby's energy.

"But there's Will."

"You have to believe Will is out here searching for his son." He glanced towards the house. "If he isn't, there's nothing you can do."

She looked at him, torn, confused.

"We should make for that other fire," he insisted. "We have to follow Toby."

* * *

Ingrid opened the studio curtains and turned off the spotlamp. The moon occupied a space between fluffy clumps of altocumulus and filled the room with a pale wash of light.

She opened the sacking bundle and took out a coil of thin copper wire. With great care she began to bind the painting tightly with the wire.

"Now, Boy, you will be bound. You will do exactly as I say."

She finished the binding and stood back, watching the painting. For a minute nothing happened. Then the painting began to tremble and shake on the easel.

Glass receptacles, containing paintbrushes, exploded on the studio shelves.

She was about to take the painting off the easel and bind it with more copper wire when the coil of wire snapped and flew through the air towards her. She threw up her arms to protect her face as the wire lashed at her.

Objects hurtled around the studio as if a tornado had burst into the place: tubes of paint, paintbrushes, palettes. The easel crashed on top of her and the painting toppled to one side.

She collapsed, motionless on the floor.

A few moments later Will, smoke-blackened, dishevelled and distraught, staggered into the studio.

"Alice? Toby?" he called. He noticed Ingrid's prostrate form and seemed about to go to her aid, but he suddenly turned and rushed distractedly from the studio.

"Alice? Toby?" he called again as he hurried away.

Ingrid stirred. Slowly she hauled herself to her feet. Her face was cut and bloody where the coil of wire had caught her.

The studio was a mess. Broken jars littered shelves. The floor was strewn with glass, paintbrushes and fractured palettes.

The painting lay face down on the moonlit floor. Ingrid was in the act of reaching for it, when all at once it flipped over and the Ghost Boy reared out.

Ingrid and the Ghost Boy faced each other.

* * *

Intense, obsessed and a little unhinged, Will hurried along the ground floor corridors of Boggarts Hall, opening doors and glancing into rooms. Each room he entered was silent, moonlit and as bereft of occupants as the last.

Quite by chance, he found the former gun room, where a number of hunting rifles were displayed in glass-fronted cabinets...

He stood still, lost in his thoughts, recalling images from his shooting days. Then he opened a cabinet, grabbed a rifle and tested the mechanism. He pulled open drawers and, after a brief search, took out a box of bullets. He checked they were the right calibre, then emptied the contents into the pocket of his Barbour jacket. Clutching the rifle, he lurched unsteadily from the room.

* * *

A barn burned in the distance. Alice and Simon rode their horses down a lane towards it.

"What is this place?" she asked, troubled. "Are there animals inside?"

He reassured her. "It's just a barn that belongs to one of the nearby farms. They just keep bales of straw in it and sometimes potatoes. No animals, as far as I know."

They approached the barn but drew rein, keeping well back. They watched as the structure swayed and collapsed with a roar and an explosion of sparks and flame.

"I can't see anyone around here," she said, shielding her eyes from the glare.

"I think we're too late," he concluded. "The Boy's moved on."

They turned and rode back down the lane.

"Over there – see!" she cried, pointing.

A third fire erupted in the darkness as they watched.

"Is it your place?" she asked.

"No, thank goodness. Mine's in the opposite direction." He sounded relieved. "Anyway, as far as I know, no one from the Hall was involved with the Boy's punishment."

"We must catch up with them," she said anxiously.

They rode away in the direction of the new outbreak of fire.

* * *

Ingrid faced the image of the Ghost Boy, whose head had reared out of the painting. He snarled and hissed at her.

She fixed her eyes on him, but was careful to keep her distance.

"Listen to what I say, Boy: you have reached the limit of your power. I command you to go back to your place of banishment!"

He laughed hoarsely, hissed and spat at her, his features contorted into a mask of hate and fury.

"You're only a phantom," she continued. "You have no power over me!"

Without taking her eyes off him she reached for a jug of water, which had somehow survived the onslaught and still stood upright on a table behind her.

"I said GO BACK!"

She flung the water at the Ghost Boy. The water appeared to scald him. He shrieked in agony and shrank back into the simple framed outline.

She seized the painting and rushed from the studio.

* * *

Stackyard buildings burned in the distance. Alice and Simon approached cautiously, keeping their horses in the lee of the nearby hedges.

"That Boy intends to burn the whole parish!" he exclaimed. "The insurance claims will be off the scale!"

She peered in the direction of the blaze. "I don't see anyone here either."

"He must be close by," he reasoned. "There are no new fires."

"There!" she cried suddenly. "See there!"

She pointed towards the edge of the burning buildings, where a figure could be seen in silhouette against the flames. They moved as close as they dared. The figure was still visible.

"It's too big for Toby," she decided.

The figure suddenly vanished.

"It could be a local," he surmised.

"No." She was adamant. "I think it was Will."

* * *

The stackyard burned in the background. Will, looking slightly deranged, appeared from the cover of a clump of bushes. He carried Simon's rifle.

His attention was drawn by movement across the field. A shadowy shape was visible in the moonlight. A human shape. Yes, definitely human.

"I've got you now, you devil!" he growled.

He shouldered the rifle and fired two rounds into

the darkness. The shape disappeared. He followed up and searched the field, looking for a body, but found nothing.

"Damnit!" he muttered under his breath. "You won't escape from me!"

He set off running across the field, oblivious of the sound of approaching fire engines. Wiping the sweat from his eyes he peered distractedly into the darkness.

* * *

Alice and Simon followed a bridleway through the fields. The full moon was hidden behind a patch of altocumulus, but there was enough diffuse light to make out field hedges and trees. If a figure had appeared ahead of them, they were sure they would have been able to follow it.

They were stunned into immobility at the spiteful crack of rifle shots.

"Was that gunfire?" she asked in alarm.

"Some crazy idiot!" he snapped angrily.

She was confused. "There's nothing to shoot at."

He pondered for a moment. "Will could have taken one of my rifles. He might think he can kill the Boy. But all he'll do is shoot Toby."

She grabbed his arm, horrified. "What can we do?"

"We'll find Toby first," he stated firmly. "We've no other choice."

* * *

Ingrid carried the painting across the stable yard to the horse trough, which stood against the stables' wall. She stopped abruptly as two shots rang out.

"Oh – the fool! He doesn't know what he's doing!" she exclaimed in dismay.

She plunged the painting into the water of the horse trough, then weighed it down with a heavy length of timber to keep it beneath the water.

She addressed the submerged painting. "Your power is done! I command you to return to your place of banishment!"

More shots sliced through the night.

"Enough of this madness!" she cried.

She hurried determinedly away among the outbuildings.

The water in the horse trough suddenly began to churn and seethe. The length of timber was tossed from the trough as if it was weightless...

The painting of the Ghost Boy bobbed up to the surface of the water.

* * *

A figure ran down a narrow lane. The running figure was at first Toby, then the Ghost Boy, then Toby again. The figure continued running, first the one, then the other, all the way along the lane.

A wind sprang up. The bushes and trees in the laneside hedges shook like demented creatures as the wind increased.

The Ghost Boy and Toby, their figures alternating, tried to cling on to laneside branches. The Ghost Boy began to materialise more strongly, Toby hardly visible at all.

"Leave me alone!" the Ghost Boy yelled.

He fought against the wind, trying to battle his way in the opposite direction.

"DAMN YOU!" he roared. "DAMN YOU ALL!"

* * *

Ingrid was hard at work in the smithy, pumping the bellows at the blacksmith's forge for all she was worth.

"Blow wind. Blow!" she cried. "Send the Boy back where he belongs! Send him back to Hob's Pond NOW!"

She stopped pumping the bellows and rushed from the building.

* * *

Will, clutching the rifle, ran into the field with the standing stone. He wiped the sweat from his eyes.

"Ah, the stone. I've found it," he muttered to himself. "I can play this magic game too!"

He approached the standing stone, circled it, then carried on running erratically down the field.

* * *

Alice and Simon left the bridleway and opened a field gate into a rough pasture occupied with gorse bushes.

He could sense her growing distress and tried to reassure her. "It's not far now. Only a few minutes from here."

She was almost in tears. "How will we know if we're in time?"

"Don't talk. Just keep moving."

"But Toby might already be..." she hesitated before uttering the word. " He might be *dead*. Will might have shot him!"

"He might. But somehow I don't think so."

They remounted their horses and moved off, winding their way through the gorse bushes.

"If Toby's alive I don't understand why there are no new fires," she wondered anxiously.

He wondered too. Either Will had destroyed all their hopes, or Ingrid's plan was working and the Boy was under control. But his intuition was telling him nothing for certain. What else could possibly have happened?

* * *

The Ghost Boy, strongly materialised, ran along an ancient hollow way overhung with hazel and elder trees. Toby was no more than a shadowy presence, appearing fleetingly and fitfully, as if he had almost ceased to exist.

The Ghost Boy emerged from the hollow way into a lane by an open field gate. As he ran past the gate four local men, dressed in dark work clothes, suddenly stepped from the bushes and grabbed him.

He was thrust roughly into a steel cage. The men fastened the cage door with a bolt, that could only be reached from outside the cage. Then they placed the cage on a litter and covered it with sacking.

"This'll finish you, you little devil!" one of the men muttered darkly.

"Geroff me! Geroff! No! NO!" the Ghost Boy yelled.

The men lifted the litter and disappeared through the gate into the field.

The Ghost Boy continued yelling as the men carried the litter through the field.

16

Will, looking dangerously disturbed, crossed the field with the rifle. The depression in the grass where Hob's Pond once lay showed up clearly in the moonlight.

He reached the fringe of bushes that surrounded the depression and lay down in the grass with the rifle to wait.

"Right, you monster!" he growled through clenched teeth, "you won't get away from me now! You won't ever get near my son again!"

He settled himself at the edge of the grassy hollow and cocked the rifle in readiness.

Ingrid appeared, walking up the field in the moonlight towards the depression once filled by Hob's Pond. As she approached the hollow it began to change...

The wind dropped. The moon broke free from the clouds and its reflection floated in the water of the pond that now occupied the hollow.

The men with the cage joined Ingrid. Together they walked towards the pond. When they were still a little way off, they removed the sacking that covered the cage.

Toby cowered in the cage, too terrified even to cry out. There was no sign of the Ghost Boy, who remained hidden.

Will stepped from the bushes, the rifle to his shoulder. "Stand back from the crate! Back I said! One of you only – one only – move forward and release my son!"

While Will's attention was focussed on the crate, one of the local men crept up behind him and knocked him down with a stunning blow. Will fell headlong in the grass, losing his grip on the rifle.

At a sign from Ingrid, the men plunged the cage into the pond. Toby and the Ghost Boy both appeared, alternating strongly.

"Dad! Mum! Help me!" Toby called in terror and desperation.

"Bastards! You're not going to beat me!" the Ghost Boy bellowed.

As the cage began to sink beneath the water Alice and Simon arrived on foot at a run. Alice grabbed Ingrid by the throat.

"You lied to me! You're murdering my son!"

Ingrid, summoning formidable physical strength, pulled Alice's hands down and thrust her away. "Get back from me! We will do what we have to! We're putting right the damage caused by your son!"

Alice barely registered Ingrid's words. Seized by panic she tried to jump into the pond. Two of the men stepped in front of her, preventing her reaching the water. She lashed out at them, but they grabbed her arms and held them firmly.

Simon turned to Ingrid accusingly. "You deceived me – why?"

She looked him squarely in the eye. "This is the only way. The boys are impossible to separate. They both live till the Boy kills his host, or they both die to this world for ever."

The cage sank deeper. Toby and the Ghost Boy started to scream, Toby in terror, the Ghost Boy in fury.

Will began to come round. He stirred and sat up. Alice spotted the rifle that had been hidden by his body. She tore herself free from the men's grasp, grabbed the rifle and pointed it at them.

"Get back!" she yelled. "I'll shoot anyone who moves!"

Ingrid tried to grab Alice from behind, but Simon restrained her. "Leave her alone!" he commanded. "Let her rescue her son!"

Toby and the Ghost Boy suddenly stopped screaming. In the appalling silence, all eyes were turned to the pond, where the cage had disappeared beneath the water.

In that brief distracted moment Will made his move and flung himself into the pond. One of the men tried to leap after him, but Alice raised the rifle and shot him in the shoulder. The other three men backed off.

After a short struggle, Will freed Toby from the cage. There was no sign of the Ghost Boy. Will hoisted Toby triumphantly on to his shoulders and waded out of the pond.

He put Toby gently on the ground. "There you are, son. You're safe."

Alice rushed up to them. "Oh, Will, that was so brave! So wonderful! I'm sorry for all my misjudgements."

Will smiled. "You're completely forgiven. What's important is that we've got Toby back safe and sound."

"Of course." She hugged them both.

Simon put his jacket around Toby's shoulders. "What amazing parents you have, young man. You should be proud of them!"

Ingrid gave them a long, silent look. She shook her head knowingly, then followed the men, who were walking away down the field, supporting their injured companion.

"You're welcome at Boggarts Hall till you sort yourselves out," Simon offered. "Not exactly five star, but better than camping out!"

* * *

Toby spent the next few days learning to ride one of Simon's ponies. He felt like himself again. The past few weeks seemed like a blur. He could remember seeing some big fires, but it was very like a dream or a film, with him just watching. One of the fires must have been his own house, but what caused it and why he was outside on his own was a mystery. And he couldn't understand why he felt so pleased while he was watching the flames.

He remembered falling into the pond. How he got there was another mystery. He must have been out walking, but he couldn't remember. Anyway, dad had rescued him and that had made everyone very happy. And the darkness had gone, as if someone had suddenly turned all the lights back on again.

But if these strange things hadn't happened, perhaps he wouldn't have got to ride Simon's pony. And that was the best thing he'd done for ages. Maybe for ever. So it had all worked out really well.

* * *

Cardboard boxes in the process of being unpacked were dumped everywhere in the rooms of Simon's vacant cottage. Alice was busy arranging books in the bookshelves. Simon had very kindly lent them most of the basics for setting up a home, plus some of his uncle's collections of poetry, a few travel books, a whole shelf of novels and even several volumes of Victorian ghost stories. She wasn't sure about the ghost stories, but in the absence of a television the books gave them something to do in the evenings while they tried to sort out the insurance and to resurrect their neglected business.

Alice's face and neck were completely healed and she looked and felt better than she had for months. She was astonished at her rapid recovery. One day she had blisters, the next day nothing. If she had been a believer in miracles, she would have said that was definitely one.

Toby passed books to her from the box on the floor. He seemed entirely normal too. She didn't talk about fires and ponds and neither did he. He showed no signs of being emotionally damaged by the past events. The possession, as far as she could tell, must have been entirely subliminal.

All Toby wanted to do was ride Simon's pony and it was all he would talk about. Lego and toy trains were things of the past. Whatever healing process

Toby needed now, the pony appeared to be providing it.

"We'll have to hurry, Mum. Simon said he'd pick us up after lunch. And we had that ages ago!"

"Don't worry. He won't be here before two o'clock. I'll be ready. I enjoy going to Boggarts Hall almost as much as you." She raised her voice slightly. "We're lucky to get this place so quickly. Simon has been such a good friend, don't you think so, Will?"

No response.

"We have to make a go of it this time," she continued. "How many chances do you get in a life?"

Silence.

"Will? You hearing me?"

She rushed into the kitchen where she had left Will unpacking the pots and pans. There was no sign of him.

"Will?" she called.

No answer.

She glanced from the window...

Will was busy in the garden. His damaged hand was now supported by a sling. He was burning the empty cardboard boxes. His eyes gleamed madly. He seemed completely unhinged.

Laughing manically, he threw a wooden chair on to the fire. More of Simon's chairs were stacked nearby, ready to burn.

The face of the Ghost Boy, like a double image, hovered for a moment next to Will's face. Alice appeared in the doorway. It took her a few seconds to grasp what was happening. Will turned to her, his voice and demeanour hideously changed.

"What the fuck are you staring at, bitch? Give me some help here!"

Ghost Boy

Alice screamed.

Dear reader,

We hope you enjoyed reading *Ghost Boy*. Please take a moment to leave a review, even if it's a short one. Your opinion is important to us.

Discover more books by Ian Taylor at

https://www.nextchapter.pub/authors/ian-taylor

Want to know when one of our books is free or discounted? Join the newsletter at

http://eepurl.com/bqqB3H

Best regards,

Ian Taylor and the Next Chapter Team

You might also like:
Dark Voyage by Helen Susan Swift

To read the first chapter for free go to:
https://www.nextchapter.pub/books/dark-voyage

Ghost Boy
ISBN: 978-4-86751-747-5
Mass Market

Published by
Next Chapter
1-60-20 Minami-Otsuka
170-0005 Toshima-Ku, Tokyo
+818035793528

9th July 2021

www.ingramcontent.com/pod-product-compliance
Lightning Source LLC
LaVergne TN
LVHW032011070526
838202LV00059B/6404